~~Objects not being fondled, May 2020~~
~~Characters (with spaces) 9,393~~

~~The Surgeon and The Archaeologist, June 2020~~
~~Characters (with spaces) 17,402~~

~~A pas de deux for an object being fondled, July 2020~~
~~Characters (with spaces) 31,115~~

~~Pas de Deux, September 2020~~
~~Characters (with spaces) 38,984~~

~~Pas de Deux, January 2021~~
~~Characters (with spaces) 50,030~~

~~Pas de Deux, February 2021~~
~~Characters (with spaces) 61,700~~

~~Pas de Deux, March 2021~~
~~Characters (with spaces) 69,100~~

~~Trying to find something to get stuck on, May 2021~~
~~Characters (with spaces) 68,883~~

~~Trying to find something to get stuck on, January 2023~~
~~Characters (with spaces) 70,842~~

~~Trying to find something to get stuck on, March 2023~~
~~Characters (with spaces) 84,156~~

~~Trying to find something to get stuck on, May 2023~~
~~Characters (with spaces) 101,699~~

~~???, July 2023~~
~~Characters (with spaces) 103,711~~

~~Body of Pieces, August 2023~~
~~Characters (with spaces) 125,480~~

Body of Pieces, January 2024
Characters (with spaces) 126,042

Body of Pieces

Joanne Masding

Bobo Books

Contents

Object list

0. It (this thing in your hands)	6
1. It (missing a bit)	10
2. It (with a nub)	16
3. It (from a grave)	22
4. It (unrigid)	30
5. It (with a face)	38
6. It (from a cave)	46
7. It (a round one)	56
8. It (that exists)	64
9. It (a performance)	74
10. It (semi-transparent)	80
11. It (in pieces)	84
12. It (mirror-like)	88
13. It (the same)	94
14. It (lumpy)	100

Plates — 107

Object index — 136

Portable portal, eked out, teased out, encouraged to sit still over leaves. But built with squiggling, wriggling love, lapping up and over edges, spilling out. Volume. Of maybe lung, or slice of liver, slotting into the space of armpit, between knees, or being gently squeezed as one might caress a sandwich and bring it to meet face. Requesting mammalian dexterity for steady flicking between bready slices, enabling total ingestion. Slow rhythms for fingers to track across. Tapping of symbols to be scanned and for magic conjuring tricks to occur inside, on pop-up screen within forehead. Rowdy thing, chattering through time. Thing with sure edges. Unit to behold, described as one of something. Speaking now as body knowledge; captured tones and emerging utterances from the fusing of an It and a who.

0. It (this thing in your hands)

I'm here.

o

I'm observing, untethered, using fictitious and bodiless eyes and ears to suck up this story, ushering it through me into description.

I'm magicking here camera-like, witnessing a parade along a series of precious Its. Flitting around each scene as a magpie, I'm collecting images, gathering actions, learning viewpoints. I'm cutting and cropping; attempting to be quick enough to catch important pieces, ingesting them, making solid.

I'm residing now in the first space, a small chunk of a volume, the antechamber. This is the way in.

There are an uncertain number of bodies, and of pieces. Two critical forms belong to beings labelled The Surgeon and The Dancer. More belong to the Its; a set of things that have emerged from the ground and stuck a corner out into the air just far enough that a toe might be stubbed on them, to be investigated further.

At this point The Surgeon and The Dancer merely know of one another, have just a blurry outline of keywords to attach to the other. They move around in occasionally overlapping circles, like a Venn diagram or orbits forming an occasional eclipse. However, each knows by the name of the other that their existing as opposing poles attached to the same centre reflects a core facet of themselves. Distance and closeness, strangers and lovers.

> *I'm joining the story partway through.*
> *You are too.*

The Surgeon and The Dancer are about to meet a set of objects, artefacts, matter. Things that have congealed into forms and been held in place long enough for us to try and know them. Each It resides in its own chamber of an unwieldy and imperfectly organised repository. It (this thing in your hands) is the first of the series; object zero, neatly demarcated into a patch of space, where it certainly is, next to elsewhere, where it definitely is not. This is an object; a tangible chunk of something, although exactly what that something is remains unclear. In the time it takes to switch from holding the back of It (this thing in your hands) while looking at the front, to feeling its inner fabric while observing its inner patterns, all manner of occurrences may have taken place.

> *I'm staying with The Surgeon and The Dancer as they go through these introductions. I'm attempting to translate the experience into a document that can time-travel into the future, that can be revisited, and slow down.*

It (this thing in your hands) hovers in the air above the foyer desk, waiting for a pair of hands to slip around its back, ready to shuffle visitors around the web of shifting and amorphous rooms.

Dynamic thing, whipping through, precise, acute, gently scribed and with graceful poise. Longness. Smooth arcs ringing out, sonorous, singing. Yet stealth-like. For both discretion and overt demonstration. Of the usual power, status, etc. Of having the most of these things. Exacting, sharp, tinny outers belie softness in the middle — softness only within the inner pattern and making and not within the overall material and execution. Its definition is hard hard hard and it's one kind of robust substance all the way through. Slinky residues of its birthing process embedded into its body. Precision of the geometric outer form built not from units of line and join and intersect, but from silky blooms of waves and tadpoles that speak of how it came to be here, with what tools, as it was enveloped, kneaded, flowed into being.

1. It (missing a bit)

I've temporarily exited the entranceway before starting proper and am instead in front of a portal through which I can see into one of its galleries. I'm hovering over The Surgeon's shoulder, floating in mid-air and watching as she sits in front of her laptop.

Unusually for The Surgeon, the laptop is on her operating table: her metal patient for today. She's pulled up a chair.

The Surgeon can't get it to fit. It's too long for her squat page. This is the first proper It that's presenting itself to The Surgeon and it needs portrait and not landscape. Trying to take this thing in begins with The Surgeon puckering a rubber glove down a trackpad in an attempt to scan its length. Even with her head tilted to the side so that her wide eyes line up with the widescreen, she can't absorb it into her and know it all at once.

I'm noting that The Surgeon's left ear is resting on her left shoulder, a frown resting above her nose.

It (missing a bit) has already been adapted to be more suited to just sitting and not meeting body parts; it's been changed from its original, full being and had parts edited out. There's a missing cushion that should offer a comfort between It's harsh edges and The Surgeon's squidgy muscle pads if ever such a wonderful occasion of holding were to occur. As it is now, even given the extra layer of support provided by the glove that's sitting baggy over the skin of

The Surgeon's hands, her flesh would meet this thing awkwardly, painfully. Both parties would have wont for a mediator, a barrier between the harshness of It's sharp form and the sack of The Surgeon's warm body that would wield it.

Knowing that she will never get to hold this It In Real Life, she fixates on the holes where a handle would once have been secured.

> *I'm looking over The Surgeon's fingers resting on the trackpad and seeing It (missing a bit) on her screen. It's bordered within a grey line, materialised as an archive pop-up and cropped to accommodate a resolution that's entirely unprocessable by human eyes. I'm seeing the image bounce up and down as she scrolls, and count a second between the top and the bottom. I'm sketching the crinkles of frustration in The Surgeon's crow's feet, noting down how the smallness of her movements as she makes this thing jump bear no resemblance to the enormity of the object and what it would take to move it as a person.*

In her head, while sitting almost motionless, The Surgeon enacts a mime with this It; pierces boundaries and forcefields, slices in, lets out, imagines that she nearly swipes through the mug of tea and cup of instant noodles that are her companions on the operating table in front of her.

Lifting it from the interface, the surgeon could take her finger, touch her nose, blink three times, and – wait, wrong magic – she's interrupted by a waft of the latex that's covering her previously highly sensitised and sensitive work tools, and which now just tap on plastic keys. She could put real finger to real artefact in her head. She imagines that she has picked up the invisible item of Important Cultural History, extends her finger out into the air in front of her nose, runs it along the It's edge. This It is all about edge. The Surgeon concentrates, meditates on where the edge is, how it would feel to meet there. She thinks she's got it, has found the bit that's it and also the bit next to it that's not, but then there's a muddling, and she finds herself back in an edgeless unspecific grey area.

> *I'm watching replays of The Surgeon acting out this interaction in the same fashion as I'm watching her just sitting there, imagining it happening in her head. I'm seeing her playing it out, and I'm seeing her remaining stationary. I'm watching it again and again with every re-reading of each sentence, and each tweaking of an edit.*

The Surgeon identifies another part of the specimen outline, this time mimes harder with it in her mind's eye, as she runs another finger along the It's icy important edge. She's sure of the same disappointing result as before, but a rushing and real response to the imagined experience crashes through her body; she clocks a raise in her heart rate and an idea of dizziness congealing in the back of her skull. Like a mandolin slicing that is already in the past before it's occurred, synapses have been fired and chemicals have been dumped to compensate. The Surgeon looks down at her gloved finger pad to inspect the new gouge that she felt get added to the topography of her middle finger. It is of course not there. She's mimed her way through some layers of mediation and arrived at the sensation in her body of an event that didn't take place.

The Surgeon is thinking more about this inning and outing. She's used to going in, turning insides into leaky, gushing outs, but less familiar with being the thing that's been gone in to, having outsides enter in order to produce an exit.

I'm zooming in to inspect The Surgeon's finger, to see the impact of this imagined interaction with such a crisp image of It (missing a bit). I'm seeing a disposable medical glove with a regular hand inside that fills my entire vision. I'm seeing no blood. I'm seeing The Surgeon use her other hand to rub her fingers, as if to double check the truth. I'm logging disappointment rather than relief.

The Surgeon files this It in screenshotted sections under Nice Things, setting it back to rest. Peeling off the old glove and stretching on a new, she gets back to the noodles with a sigh.

Important, tiny plain adorned with glowing crevices; glistening rivers of negative space to be imparted into a right material for mapping, holding. Singing brightness, multiplying light beams and choral pools. Slipping off again, ready again. Speaking a vital message. Form for recording voice, calling out. Nub of lump on reverse. Growth for gripping to be airborne and articulate, so that it might do the thing that it does. Preeeesssssssssss. Body onto nub into gloop onto sheet into eyes and eyes and minds. But never anymore. Never will acidic, oily fingers leak corrosive juices onto highly polished body. No longer will it absorb warmth of anything, lest its innards jiggle too excitedly and wobble out of place, lest its hardness be in fact softness and it wear away into nothing. No more dipping into anything and imparting traces of glorious arcs onto something else. Tannoy made mute.

2. It (with a nub)

I'm progressing from my earlier position and moving beyond the antechamber to the inside of the archive proper. I'm seeing The Dancer in here with me, but I'm not sharing her viewpoint as I did previously with The Surgeon. Instead of seeing what she sees I'm seeing her at work, observing her as she gets closer to the bundle of atoms that is the second It of the set.

This It is really trapped. Lost in shadows. Grey carpet squares, greyer walls, a column of lift shaft strategically placed in the sight-line to block a good view of this It from afar. It's all chevron forward, chevron backward, X not that way. Spin around, zoom out, lost it altogether. Shiny speck in the corner. Glare of spotlight on glass cabinet. Glare of spotlight on tiny golden chunk. Glare of spotlight on resolution too low to see any details but from other photos it looks like a glowingly delicious morsel.

Unlike The Surgeon, poised from her perch and with only a doorway open onto the inside, The Dancer has slid into the insides of the object repository. She's found an access point that offers a way of being up close; she's gone beyond the surface to a space of inhabitation. Motives remaining murky, she's mooching about, waiting for something to brush her eye, curious as to what it might be.

Fingers making twinkling shapes in the air, The Dancer tickles away at the layers that It (with a nub) is sat beneath. She works to discard the layers of unnecessary noise, knowing that a block of an It is there in the middle, buried under weighty coatings of glass casings, taxonomic discrepancies, Google voodoo, cultural burdens. Sweeping through the detritus, she locates something solid.

> *I'm watching the lightness of The Dancer as she teases away film after film from the It, seeing her lithe form slip under unhindered, moving within the grey backdrop, the object so tiny as to be almost non-existent to my eyes.*

Now that this object has been somewhat revealed to The Dancer, from her prized vantage point of being up close and inside the museum with all human faculties at her disposal, she peers on, sweeps on, gets ready to meet the artefact with her all. She pauses and turns accountant for a moment, pondering how many units of cultural and historical significance she's just unearthed. This is a good one. Major asset. It's front, back and inside are uniformly solid golden culture honey.

> *I'm witnessing from across the room the moment that The Dancer unearths the gleaming It (with a nub), hailed to me by a siren of light striking off it as she opens it to the air.*

As she is dusting off a final layer of debris a nugget shines out.

It (with a nub) is now revealed to The Dancer in its entirety, and she lets the fleeting assessment of monetary worth drip off it. She is right up next to it, breathing the same air, joyfully being her being in parallel with the It joyfully being its being.

> *I'm feeling slinky in her joy.*

I'm being temporarily deposited in front of a phone video playing over in The Dancer's mind, as this It reconnects her to her first awareness of the existence of Charidotella sexpunctata, the Golden tortoise beetle, scuttling its unearthly, shining, brilliant metallic dome on a five-second loop. Metallic elytra clicking open and shut, reflecting wonder on repeat.

As she wiggles in happiness while surveying her find, she has the realisation that her body poses a problem. The It, while sitting immediately in front of her, occupies a multi-dimensional lump of the universe and The Dancer can only look/feel/taste from her one plane in space. She can't know the back when she's knowing the front, and the under-surface poses yet more mysteries.

Luckily The Dancer is well versed in spatial choreographies. She changes tack from the me-you thing-not dichotomy, and instead accepts the extracted channels in the surface of this It as an invitation to slither down. She climbs onto the It, stretches herself around and through its delightful patterns, understands the velocity of its gift, gets to know its curves with her own.

I'm watching The Dancer happily wind her body around the surface grooves of this It, seeing her learn how the lump on the reverse can be mapped with her lumber spine, seeing her slip off again returning to the ground, climbing on once more to make another wonderful lap.

The thing with this It is that we don't know what it's trying to say. It is agreed that it is speaking and that what it utters is important, but the message is mainly lost. When this It is used (not that it will be), it actions symbols too old, too ambiguous, too forgotten to be totally legible. Outdated codes and no-longer-spoken lexicons. A dialect from a region that can't be found. The Dancer knows it differently. She knows from inside of it that it is important, is beautiful, is highly significant, valuable, old, gleaming, culturally stupendous, historically momentous, but also that it's a murky thing. She knows that this is what it is saying.

Returning to her feet after her slip-sliding, The Dancer brushes herself off. Tiny airborne flecks from her clothing are illuminated briefly, origin and destination unknown, uncared about. She puts the artefact back where it was and leaves it as she found it.

Discard changes, do not even save a copy.

An It borrowing from bodies. Head-like, belly-like, lip-like, womb-like, mouth-like. For nestling into. Modelled on cupped palm catching rain, embrace gripping sack, skull safely holding a brain. Pushed out of itself. Birthed from a blob and with enough wherewithal to catch its new identity and hold it in place. The taste of dry bones being baked in. An arid and brittle being, yet a mouth meeting it would be sucked in; moistures magnetised to its belly. The trail of a caress from a tongue, a dribble of miss-sip, would leave a map of marks on its skin. Patterns of porosity until they float away. A form to be animated, mobile and busy in living, passed among many, with flat patch for being left aside, put under gravity's arrest and told to be still. Ovaries and ovoids and eggs.

3. It (from a grave)

The Surgeon is still in her theatre, at her laptop, gazing through the window onto the archive. She's strolling the still hallways, passing occasional pixelated blobs on plinths on either side. Two clicks north, drag left, scroll on, and so on. She passes an arrow labelled 'Romans'.

> *I'm finding myself positioned at the back of The Surgeon's head, seeing her long hair falling down her back and the shape of her cranium underneath, framed by the out-of-focus, illuminated screen in front of her. I'm trying to discern if she knows what she's doing, and am unsure. I'm feeling her sense of dislocation, of searching for a means of navigation that's other to what she has known before.*

As is always the case when churning up the clayey earth body of this continent, there is the release of a background noise of Roman remains to contend with. Roman castoffs are strewn throughout the majority of the mass that moves under the grass and tarmac. Endless litter of empire. What to do with it all? Progressing her quest for something not yet defined, and using her shovel cursor to excavate and sift through the chunks that appear on her screen, The Surgeon is filing the lumps of debris that are vomited up into a yellow Warning folder.

Flicking through Roman image lump after Roman image lump, The Surgeon trips on a deceptively big piece of artefact and stumbles, scooting the image on her screen to somewhere unknown. It places her now on the edge of a muddy-bottomed pit of bits; pieces and parts and shards and chips that are all laid out across the dirt with the anatomical precision decreed by the archive catalogue. The slip must have sent her down an unseen corridor or goods lift, to an active hole in the museum basement, bringing in artefacts straight out of the ground.

> *I'm switching to Surgeon-eye-view after the jolt of her getting stuck on something. I'm looking out of her face across the hoard and examining an array of pieces laid out on the brown across her screen.*

The slipping has brought The Surgeon to a pile of individual pieces of brokenness, each of them a single unit in their own right but equally just a fraction of something more. Her eye gets caught on a splendid and pleasing curl of something – the next It of the collection – and she allows it to magnify and fill her viewfinder. She wants it to encompass her entirely, wonders how much further she could go, how much more inside this thing she might be able to get.

Scrubbed up, fingers poised, The Surgeon begins the rehearsed and sacred process: forefinger pad meet thumb pad; pair of digits rest on trackpad; mime them apart as if prising open a tiny orifice; lift away from surface; repeat until burrowed in as far as necessary.

The Surgeon is initially thrilled by her efforts in magnification, believes that she may have actually gone so far in as to reach just beyond the visible surface and arrive at the inside. But wait, not yet. Instead she's been met with an external plane of sandy red and hasn't found a way inside the It at all. No hollow interior, no delightful cavern, no romantic hollow, no sumptuous, ringing darkness. Just pushed up tight against a dry, scratchy outer.

I'm sighing with her at this passing flicker.

The Surgeon reverses her zooming manoeuvres to return to her pit-side view, to be met with conflicting sensations of both pleasure and irritation as she eyes a figure in the pit with the splendid and pleasing It. Not stuck out on the edge with her, it's The Dancer, who is somehow able to be rolling around as one of the pieces, nestled right in among them. (Gently) bumping and grinding among them.

Unaware of being observed, The Dancer dips towards It (from a grave) as it rests in the hole alongside the array of other artefacts. She meets it. The Surgeon watches as the female form moving on her screen pushes her softness against the hardness, press-moulding herself against it so as not to spill out of any gaps. There's no room for anything to escape, just a lovely snug nestling, lip to lip, mouth to mouth. In to in to out to out. Transfixed by this dance between woman and chunk of stuff, The Surgeon wonders how she too can get access to this plane of delicious and joyful nuzzling.

I'm flitting between looking onto the static It (from a grave) from The Surgeon's distant viewing station and looking around a mobile It (from a grave) from within The ~~Archaeologist's~~ Dancer's immediate touching plane. I'm feeling a variety of kinds of longing seeping from, and pointing towards, the three players of the scene.

More about The Dancer should be divulged than what has been outlined so far, to build up a sense of her in more dimensions. She's right on the cusp. Currently nulliparous but not for long, she is full to bursting with her firstborn and is a big, taut mass that's struggling to readjust to its shifting centre of gravity.

> *I'm seeing now this shifting in The Dancer, how she is not one and not quite two. I'm thinking about how it feels to be this way, how it feels to have a body that swells and ebbs, to be with something that is yours and not yours, to have a body that's a brain, that has another brain, to be in the world as a body and not as an anonymous floating head. To be something so big.*

In her search for another kind of understanding, the bit The Surgeon wants to know is the bit that isn't the surface body but the inner body; the space for inhabitation. She doesn't want just hardness slammed against another hard shell, she wants to access contours. She desires gentle curves, seductive cupping, turning and admiring from all angles.

> *I'm getting stuck with her at the outer, at the protective case.*

The Dancer, full as she is, still meets this object gracefully. Their pairs of spheres mirroring, she first bounces into it, like grapes in a bunch, and it impresses into her, gently displacing her fleshes and liquids around its body.

> *I'm taking a moment here. I'm pausing.*

The Surgeon removes her tongue.

!

!

She's just taken it out.

Holding the panting floppy end with one hand and precision-cutting tool pinging off beams of operating-table light on the metal with the other, she has liberated her taste organ from her mouth.

As easy as that.

Rooted to her spot in the operating theatre, and stuck with frustration at having just her eyes as her means of exploration, The Surgeon fell back on the process most familiar to her and made an edit to her form. She understood that shifting the reach of her borders could help her to better decode what she was being presented with. Newly armed with a secondary piece of herself, one that could be outside of the main bit of her, perhaps now she will be able to find a new kind of articulation.

I'm residing in The Surgeon's chest, feeling her – not overly rapid – breathing in and out. I'm finding an awareness of her heart beating somewhat faster than usual. I'm not understanding the sensations occurring within her mouth but I'm remembering the iron-heavy taste of blood. I'm feeling her life-and-death assuredness at the situation.

The Surgeon holds her tongue between gloved fingers, watches as it flip-flops to and fro, a curious, boneless, slug-like creature, created by her, birthed by her, and her new tiny twin. Now airborne and with a far greater sphere of reach than when attached to her face, The Surgeon unfolds her arm and draws a circle through the air around her, sucking up tastes from the space just beyond her fingertips. She wipes it across the surface of the screen in front of her, choosing a classic window-wiping motion; diagonal swipes from top-middle to bottom-left, moving gradually east.

Her laptop absorbs none of her tongue's saliva, in fact actively repels it, instead leaving rainbow traces of spit droplets as they refract the artificial light. There's so much sheer-edgedness here, there's no knowledge of curvature. There's no delicately imperfect topography of a surface made by a hand, just plain old flatness.

Returning to her screen, The Surgeon runs her piece of tongue over the cushioning information that's presented next to It (from a grave) where it lays in its pit. How to absorb facts into an actual bodily experience? Through smashing it into a dismembered body part? She tastes: text, sticks of letters, loops of serifs, lumpy grammatical objects, 'from a grave'. She continues to mash her fleshy stub onto the glass-like surface and traces the three lines that come together to make the shape of an A, noting how the spaces around the edges of this It slot in so tidily to form a neatly tessellating mosaic.

I'm facing her screen and floating around The Surgeon's negative spaces, following the air flowing under her lower arm on top of the keyboard, the nook under curled fingers. Even with the unplanned surgery and her quest for something new, I'm being repeatedly taken back to The Dancer: The Surgeon can't take her eyes off her.

The Surgeon is taken out of this moment by a blue bottle that ricochets by, tacking, tapping, ticking off the windowpane, mug, door frame, and fizzing for a time behind the semi-opaque blinds. She thinks about it in proximity to her open oral wound, considers how since she noticed its presence it has managed three times to narrowly avoid the partially open door it entered through. She should've followed the recommendations and taped it up after all. Returning to face her workstation, The Surgeon sees It (from a grave) reclining in its pit, and The Dancer too, nestled up against it, probably tired from her efforts, fallen asleep.

Over under
over under
over under over under over under over under. Seems the same, but within the over under are notation-defying gaps and silences. With pauses. Time spent hidden from surface and time spent on show. A code of on and off, strands of binary information ticking out a surface rhythm.
New line.
To protect a border. Withstander for both delicate surface needing shielding from weights, roughness and labour underneath, and lumping, chafing, eroding load on top.
New line.
Made of pieces. Pieces of long thin wiggled together to form new long thin, wiggled together to form new plane of a thing, to form this It. One thing, made of one kind of thing. Speaking of instructions and map reading, follow line on line, count the lines, count the gaps, build it up into a sheath to hide under and a tent to shut out. A scarecrow's drawing of a body to keep warm in the field, keep the birds off.
End.

4. It (unrigid)

The fans on The Surgeon's computer are working hard, whirring loudly. Expending energy to cool down seems counterintuitive, but if it can work for sweaty, glandy bodies it can work for machines with too many tabs running too many simultaneous museum walkthroughs, Zoom, 24-hour news, Twitch, Slack, bang, wallop.

The Surgeon is still in theatre, still at her operating table, still questing on through her laptop trying to make sense of bodies and objects and knowing, still clutching her severed tongue in one hand. With the white noise-like spinning-fan song as a backdrop, The Surgeon has paused in front of the fourth object: It (unrigid). Whether it is coincidence that has brought the two women together, to the same room, to the same artefact – one of many hundreds of thousands in the repository – or the design of a convenient story, The Dancer is there with it too. The Surgeon watches The Dancer like she watches the It; jealous and in wonder and wanting.

> *And I'm watching them all, again watching longing. I'm feeling for The Surgeon as she struggles with her head and her thoughts all ballooning out and getting stuck in front, and feeling awe for The Dancer as she lives with an effortless being and knowing and ok.*
>
> *I'm looming over It (unrigid), this time watching birds-eye. I'm seeing the top of The Dancer's head moving into frame stage-right, edges of the room marking the crops of my field of vision.*

The Dancer comes to stand aside this probably floppy It. This portion of the collection centre is bright white all over, bar a few words attached to the floor along the front edge. There is little extraneous space around the edges of It (unrigid) that's laid on the white ground.

The Surgeon watches too. She wonders how she should know what to do with it. How to know how special it is. How to know whether, if she were to handle it, she must – according to insurance, conservation, general policy – don particular branded gloves and reverently lower it onto a cleansed sheet within a climate-controlled vault, or if she could just pop it in a carrier bag and be on her way. Not that either of those options are available to her in this moment, from this distance. Here, the thing is placed, made to rest gracefully. It looks old, but not decrepit, not brand spanking new, not clean and shiny. It speaks of care. But it's also full of holes. It has intentional holes for arm, leg, head, tail; and intentional holes for needle, thread, stitch, gap between; and other kinds of holes that The Surgeon doesn't know where to fit within the taxonomy she's just made up that might include holes for history, geography, functionality, personality.

> *I'm feeling a quiver of fun ripple through The Surgeon as she allows curiosity, so often dampened by the weight of statements and facts, to bubble up and play.*

Giving up this train of thought, The Surgeon finds that The Dancer has lain down and rested herself on top of this It, mapped her body to its. Mirroring its placing, she's become geometric, all perpendicular limbs, scarecrow-like, jarring with her usual preference for supineness. As well as a love of dancing, The (appropriately named) Dancer, also has a love of lying down. Alongside the anticipated shift in moving and prancing that's necessary while pregnant, The Dancer is also getting used to an unanticipated change in the ways that it is comfortable, and even permitted, to curl up and rest while with child. Some lying-down postures that her two bodies could accept are listed as dangerous, likely deadly, by people like The Surgeon. She's added these things to her mental list of rules one must adhere to in order to attempt to birth a thing.

But It (unrigid) doesn't want to follow the needs of The Dancer's bodies, it wants hers to follow its.

Breaking further with protocol, The Dancer awkwardly flops her nested bodies off the It, picks the thing up, and climbs inside it. She encourages it to flex itself over her model of a body and fills its insides. She recognises it as another cloche to add to the collection of containers for discrete parts and processes that she is formed out of and gives form to. Cell edge here, organ boundary there, skin-covered outer, enamel wearing away, sock holding a foot.

She twirls in it, then settles back down on the floor to rest.

> *I'm zooming back out to portal-view at the operating table and feeling The Surgeon's furrowed brow settling lightly back into place, fun curiosity bubble meeting wanting, yearning chagrin.*

The Surgeon rotates her laptop away from a shard of sunlight that's entered stage-left so as not to become taken once again out of the moment by the sea of dust particles that are illuminated on her screen. While this pretence at cleanliness is certainly preferable to being blinded, it highlights to The Surgeon her own lack of agency; no amount of swivelling of her physical self in her room up here equates to any actual mobility around the It in the round down there. She's still still at the other end, still looking at the same flat face-edge of data.

Annoyed with herself for losing focus, but going along with it anyway, The Surgeon's eyes scan the text labels that are glued onto the floor below the base-edge of the object. She picks out words including real, crafted, traditional, forced into poverty. Forced into poverty. She doesn't have tools for dealing with such words, and wonders if she should be thankful for the particular conditions of oppression and destitution that enabled such a beauty to be borne, or was that not what they meant? Eyes continuing on, The Surgeon becomes distracted again by the artefacts' visual poetry and gets caught on a particularly beautiful area of patterning that erases the fleeting and vague sense of discomfort she felt at learning of the maker's suffering.

> *I'm sticking with The Surgeon, and sticking with my view onto the same portal of white, seeing It (unrigid) pasted over The Dancer but still neatly framed within the room.*

After her initial trials with It (from a grave), for the time being The Surgeon has put her tongue to one side and gone back to using eyeballs as her primary means of exploration. She's wondering how else she might try to get inside this one. How to be more like The (beautiful) Dancer. How to know it differently. In a somewhat clumsy and overwrought proposition, The Surgeon thinks that one way to know this It differently would be to build up a topography of the object by imagining herself shrunk down, and making a map of it by following along the edges of its many stranded parts using the pencil and paper waiting on her shelf. She could draw out the lines that slot together to form its malleable body by travelling along its ridges and valleys, making a flimsy version right here that she could hold. It would be like following the illuminating probes in keyhole surgery. She begins, and quickly halts. The edges of the paper arrive too quickly. They don't talk easily to the size of her body. She tries again. She thinks about translating the object, this time instead into an equivalent notation of readable quavers, rests and bars that she could extract from the patterning and take inside herself through her ear canals. The lack of perspective offered by her static viewpoint makes this a non-starter. If only she could ask The Dancer what to do.

Instead, The Surgeon asks herself if she's the kind of person who navigates by borrowing a bird's eye, orienting herself with a map formed from above, or if she's the kind of person that moves at street level, memorising lists of left, right, second-left, end. When performing surgery she's certainly a bird, but out in the world she's more of a rat, travelling along the streets to build up a map that she can follow around in real time. She imagines recreating this It in her lap by forging through its channels and abrupt endings. She skids virtually along the strand-like roads, taking turnings as her urges present themselves.

I'm feeling progress inside The Surgeon's body with these actions, sensing a small but noticeable inflation in her bank of body knowledge, a softening of her tense shoulders.

I'm moving to face The Dancer, taking her in as would a full-length mirror, with It (unrigid) pasted over most of her.

Comfortable with the collection of tools at her disposal for navigating around the repository and knowing the things within it, The Dancer enjoys her inhabitation within this thing. Like the fullness and tautness in her belly, she feels a rightness with being inside it. Another blanket means more safety, more comfort. She moves her limbs to know where it pulls, shifts her weight around inside the object, feels it brush against her bump.

After some gentle swaying and inching around, The Dancer has the realisation that she is in fact now confined to the insides of this It. She can't peel it off herself; doing so would require shapes that her body can't access at this point in this trimester. She's not averse to the thought of having been swallowed whole and resigns herself to her newly applied skin. It is a very beautiful new outer, and any energy to do anything else about it is being sucked up from within.

The Surgeon watches from above as The Dancer exits stage-right into darkness, her body still clad in this mightily special It. How can she find a gap, a place to slip a finger in and know them both?

Old money, antique gold, inherited wealth. Ribbles and nodules of dull gleaming surround a flat and cornered evenness with shapes floating on top. Parenthesis pedestal orbits the inner space. Leads one into, challenges one not to ogle at, to get to the main event. Representation of a body stepping out from earthy light. Silky puckering and glossy unfolding stepping out from a representation of body. Intricates, curls, sheens, decadences. Slippy trick of sleight of hand, form void of substance, volume bereft of weight. No reaching in to reassure with a touch on a wrist. Wave empty palm in front of blank face to get attention. Be met with glazing outwards. Closer inspection of stick-figure provokes tiny caresses to appear. Hues of sap licked on by feather stroke, vibrating as a swarm, barely holding together to prolong the mirage.

5. It (with a face)

Platform game. Ready player 1.

> *I'm resting at head height, following The Dancer who is navigating the space ahead, working her way towards It (with a face). She's moving, light and easy on her feet.*

This game, on this level of the museum, begins with The Dancer at one end of a light and airy room. Yellowy bright rather than white, and with lots of surface textures and materials for light to bounce across. Brightness bounces around having entered through grand windows and pouring out of endless ceiling spotlights. Everything here is face on and flatly arranged. It (with a face) isn't the only special thing to reside in this room; it is one of many lined up, and awaiting adoring stares. There are no jaunty angles, it's perpendicular heaven; a parallel dream of pure fronts and backs. The awkward bits that surely exist – fixings, edges, sockets, services – don't catch on The Dancers' eyeballs here. As long as she keeps her blinkers in place, ignores the rest of her that holds her eyeballs up, she can know the artefacts in this platform game from their dead-on sweet spots.

There are learnable characters within this gallery that The Dancer must appease in order to progress and meet It (with a face). First is *lump with a slot*, then comes *clear plane slipped in*. The It, and others like it, are then affixed to, and meet their publics on, the front surface of the *clear plane slipped in*.

I'm taking in this scene that has the most amount of information I've experienced so far in the story. There are a multitude of devices at work, of forms, shapes and matter, each gripping tight to an important artefact. There's been no helpful cropping and editing to elevate the critical It, the sifting is still to be done.

I'm wondering where The Surgeon is, if she exists while I'm working up a bit without her, still hunting and testing through her portal.

Clear plane is very much visible and very much trying not to be, making an attempt at ghostliness. These are particularly clumsy ghosts; while transparent, their slippy fronts reflect too much of the light that pings about, quickly giving away their location. The depth of their transparency, too, so definitely describes their weight, solidity and magnitude, like ice sculptures to be leapt over. Unlike the Its that The Dancer and The Surgeon have been meeting and trying to meet so far, these props give themselves up too easily.

And the props aren't even the things to be talking about; they're just the scenery, the lead up, a bit more construct dribbled out from the floor and off walls to support the special things.

Lump with the slot is a more honest persona; a simple unit of weight that offers counterbalance and a giant signpost to the It. It's as if the prized object might be missed if *lump* wasn't there, or that a more delicate and discrete solution would be too puny to do the job. Or that the ghostly trick played by *clear plane* might fool The Dancer so satisfactorily that she would walk right on through and bounce right off this valued It. It probably has to do with insurance.

I'm pacing alongside The Dancer as she traverses the rows and columns. I'm feeling the assuredness in her feet.

The Dancer is led onwards by her clear internal compass, stepping forward along a straight line, the tiles covering the floor counting her strides. She works her way into the body of the room, passing other aisles of things on props. With sidesteps she navigates along a horizontal avenue, ignoring yet more valuable items, until she arrives at the coordinates she somehow knows are correct, and comes to rest facing It (with a face) head on. Her eyes track up and over the *lump* at her feet, almost obscured by her own bulging body, then skirt along the pretence of the see-through *clear pane* resting in its slot, and finally she reaches the It.

I'm looking right out of her eyes.

Or has she? There's another lovely bit of coy faff. A new bumpy and lustred float that's more akin to the It than *clear plane*, but isn't wholly part of its true body proper. A golden surround, knobbed on four corners. It's ribbed (for her pleasure), one last bit of anticipation before the main event; object foreplay. Training her eyes not to wander too far, too fast, she knows that it will be better if this part is drawn out. The Dancer cranes her head up close, lifts an outstretched forefinger, and looks just at what she can see in the space immediately surrounding it. Her shimmering, two-tone *Aqua Mermaid Moonfish* nail varnish glints at her. It needs some touching up. She watches herself as she hovers a finger above a series of gilt studs and then finally, delightfully, she's almost at the edge and about to reach it.

The Dancer pauses her charming hand mid-air, then let's herself nudge her finger to graze the edge and meet the precious surface of this It daringly with her body. She has to adopt an unusual leaning pose so that her protruding baby doesn't get prodded; neither of them is ready for that. Lightly, her finger meets a flat surface, with not much to report except a texture of slickness, and a resulting mild friction against her gentle sweeping. She tries to remain in her fingertip, but her eye is called beyond into an area of depthy, expansive light, that has jostling within it all manner of textures and forms to swim over. There are more structural tricks for The Dancer to unfurl. Cooped up within the flatness is a boundless depth. Cubic units of pictorial space. She pauses.

Realising that this flat place is not the realm where finger works its magic, The Dancer steps back as she considers her next move. This change in viewpoint reveals to her that within this flat and yet terribly good-sized portal is – not unusually – a gloriously average specimen of a middle-aged unknown white male. Adorned, as we have come to expect, with silky billowy flowy glory.

She places the back of her hand on the front of this It, her hand maintaining contact with the surface as she shifts her open palm across to meet the delicate hands of the man-shape in front of her. Nails curved safely away of course, she might be flouting the no petting rules but she's not an animal. Proportionally he's as big as her, but given all his props and extensions and artificial limbs he towers on his podium and gazes into the middle distance above her head. His expression announces that he wields the power to be disinterested.

I'm exiting The Dancer's body and panning to the side, seeing The Dancer and It (with a face) look at one another. I'm catching something beginning to glint in her eye. It's not the love and longing and frustration I saw in The Surgeon earlier, but it's as powerful.

The Dancer pauses in front of this latest object, feels something stirring. Maybe she is an animal after all. She doesn't feel a primal rousing in her depths from sheer beauty or awe or sublime overwhelm, but this It has awoken something. Her hackles are raising, prickling against the previously encountered It (unrigid) that she realises now she is still wearing; a poised fury swells up inside her, an historical, ancient moving, sickness-like.

Stop.

I'm cutting suddenly to The Surgeon, holding her usual seated position, surveying straight ahead, hands fiddling between keys and trackpad. Has she been watching this whole time?

The Surgeon knows that she's missed something. She registered something that went by too quickly, that she couldn't absorb and decipher in real time but which almost certainly occurred. She scoots back in fifteen-second intervals and waits for the buffer to buffer.

The Surgeon is prone to distractions. Bluebottles, things in the middle distance, they carry her away like a feather on a pond. This time it's a scab. She has no accessible details of how she cut the skin on the back of her left hand, but she has the neat, chewy memory imparted into her flesh, describing that it occurred.

With a nail she picks at its corner, passing time with her impatient waiting. It gives the right amount of resistance so as to be pleasing; requires some effort to move but begins to lift away, and still provokes a tangible sensation in the hand that's being left behind. With a sting it comes off fully, and she's left holding a tiny bit of herself in her fingers. Almost of her fingers. She notes that it's not much of a production miracle to behold, not much of a birthing to celebrate.

I'm inspecting the collection of dried cells clinging to one another up close on The Surgeon's finger. I'm feeling her wondering how she got to this point, this place, all the decisions she made and didn't make. There's a version of the flow chart where she could have been a dancer instead. Or a mother.

Loading complete and scab casually flicked aside, The Surgeon is watching a re-run of the scene from the beginning. She observes The Dancer enter stage-front, as if she has emerged from the audience and walked directly onto the stage. The Dancer walks out from underneath The Surgeon's eyeline. She moves down the rows then across the columns. She sees her arrive in front of it; watches as she skims over the *lump, clear plane* and the border. The Surgeon is studying as The Dancer, earlier artefact still spread across her back, runs her finger from a place beyond the object to its outside surface, pauses, and then slips the back of her hand across its front. The recording of a woman's hand meeting the hand shape depicted in the It plays out in front of The Surgeon. She's focused and waiting. Then she's caught by the sensation of a ruby of blood forming on her own hand where the scab should still be. She feels the twitch of a trickle about to run down her wrist. Instinctively, The Surgeon puts the back of her hand to her tongueless mouth.

And now again she's missed it, she's left with only the aftermath: a video of a seething and breathless woman in front of an image of an unmoved and indifferent man.

Total pitch-blackness. Hovering within a crust of pixelated snakeskin. Sweeping around, looping up. Cyclonic wrapping and creeping north, up the Z-axis in three dimensions minimum.
Interlocking personified. An interlocking. Interlocutor. Inflated force field. Maybe shaped by water, lapped into a whirlpool and bottomed out or bottomed across to pull the whole together into one.
Dynamism in the snakeskin, in the repeated rows of overlaid scales, nestled and stacked and locked into place. But skin-like — as in tonal layers that coat and hold innards in — it is not. The skin is its entirety. A thicker skin, more processed, more specific, leather-like, with chewy depth, with noise and chunkiness in its moving, with volume. But leather-like — as in sack that is one plane peeled off and shaped around another, uniform, smooth, claggy — it is not. This leather is multitudinous, is pliable, buildable; and grows in many parts that push out cling together make a dam, tap out a rhythm that is this It.

More voids hollowed out from womanly bodies. Gentle cavern bearing curves and coils.

6. It (from a cave)

I'm sitting with The Surgeon, feint cars, lorries, ambulances vibrating through the air. I'm feeling her tiring of these tangos and of being stuck again out here, still sat just looking at her screen. I'm wondering when there will be some progress.

There's a scale at the bottom of the enlarged picture that's pasted across the entirety of her laptop screen, with chunks of black-and-white demarcating units. It's a picture of the next It: It (from a cave). The Surgeon counts that the width of It (from a cave), resting above the ruler, is less wide than 10 units. She's not used to this need for transposition, she usually works just with what she's given as it is, body to body, 1:1.

With a lack of any better ideas, The Surgeon follows the same full-scale approach. Working full-size body-scale she picks up a mug that was resting on a set of terribly non-sterile scalpels that are standing in as her coaster. She takes the mug as her single unit; a body-double for the object that sits out of reach. Wishing the image on the screen onto the reality more closely in front of her, she takes her off-white, slip-cast mug and forces It (from a cave) onto it.

I'm viewing the scene from behind The Surgeon's head again. I'd be unable to draw The Surgeon's mugshot, but I can feel what it's like to be her forehead, eye sockets, jaw. I'm seeing her as a silhouette, illuminated at her workstation; screen, image, mug-hand, face. She's trying.

Held up to the screen, The Surgeon's mug and the image of It (from a cave) flashing up behind it are almost the same size: they could likely both, within their exterior boundaries, contain a woman's fist. Clenching loosely, she puts her fist inside the mug, feeling what it's like to be contained in part in a space that size. She notices the dull ping of her first finger knuckle as it's stopped by the ceramic base, and the cool of the glassy glaze against the outside edge of her palm and the top section of her thumb. The rest of her hand feels nothing except itself. She repeats the experiment a few times to consolidate the data. Remove hand from mug, push fist in. Pull out. Push in. Out. In. Out. In. With this new knowledge in her hand she goes back to eyeing the object on her screen. The Surgeon acts out the in-out-in with the mug, this time also pushing and pulling it through the image, the textures and tones so different to one another. Through the attempt at overlapping, she feels older memories in her skin returning; a brush against an armchair in a sunny conservatory, a childhood splinter from a shaggy fence panel. But try as she might, through this flimsy prop there's no way of her pinpointing the exact sections of hand and the specificity of the sensations from human nerve-endings over physical textures that she would be able to process if she were able to fist this It for real.

One hand still wedged in the mug, The Surgeon reaches down beside the mattress that's conveniently right next to her operating table workstation, and grabs a textbook. It begins as a reach out to steady herself, a swipe out with the hope of finding a hand to hold hers and help her on her way (ideally it would be The Dancer's hand that met hers), but she's met only with a volume of papers. Grabbing the book, and with only that grabbing hand available for manipulating it, she rests it on her lap and flicks through from back to front as if it were a flipbook. At the corners of the pages, individual letters conflate over one another into a sequential squiggle. The moving glyphs shift into empty shapes. Although her most familiar mode of comprehension, The Surgeon feels it unlikely that letters could be the best means we have for making sense of everything that's in this world. The best way of taking things in and expressing others out.

Cascading on from this thought, The Surgeon is transported by recalling a small bird form she used to know. It was a glorious, slippery, silky, glowing thing and a dweller in a favourite nearby museum. She tries to hold it solidly in her mind in front of her, but the giant signposts that were stuck onto this delicate form, that also reside in her memory, pull her aside. Scrawls of 'made of XX', 'born in XX', 'used as XX', sweep her up and whisk her out of the bird's body, to falsified places built up from GCSE history books and global period dramas. These are not the words she needs. The Surgeon isn't looking for the envelopes of facts that are licked on after, she needs the voice of the inside that can bring closeness, empathy with clay, likeness between stomach and wood. She needs the knowledge of a dancer.

> *I'm watching these memories too, being transported from one museum to another, in front of recollections that forge endless new versions. I'm struggling to remember where I started.*

The Surgeon can't see The Dancer fully at this moment, but the ends of her limbs and the bump of her baby ping occasionally into view from just out of shot, alive beyond the rectangular window. The Surgeon wants to get closer to The Dancer as well as to all the Its. She wants The Dancer to show her how to use her body without the need for tools and technical appendages and textbooks.

I'm enjoying the glimmer of a swollen ankle retracting into the wings. I'm wondering whether The Dancer is enjoying performing too, if she does know we're watching.

The Surgeon puts a headphone earbud into each ear. She sits like this for a moment listening to the new noises she can hear when she taps her fingertips onto her own head. Surely that's something The Dancer would do.

In a rare moment of not thinking, The Surgeon unmutes her microphone and shrieks out into the world. She hears her own cry returned to her ears and becomes aware of the loop running through the different orifices of her head. From within her throat the balloon of noise rises up and falls out of her mouth, bounces over the nearby wall and pile of books beside her and recoils into her ear and head. Simultaneously she feels the vibrations that take the shortcut; that go directly from her throat, flopping over the stump of her tongue, that tunnel their way through solids, liquids, to brain.

She is making noise.

Beginning with the most basic option, with just letting out whatever sounds she can find, The Surgeon tries making any kinds of noises that will reach out. Yells, whoops and amorphous shouts.

I'm noting that The Surgeon is shouting an array of noises, but I'm not hearing them through my own ears. It's like trying to remember the smell of bacon – I know that I know what it is, but I can't outline it with any certainty. Rather that I'm understanding that the noise is coming out of her.

I'm feeling her euphoria in my mouth at this bold and thoughtless act of creation.

Hunching closer to her screen, and suddenly aware of the blurred edge of her nose peeking out ahead of her, The Surgeon begins to translate into description the It (from a cave) that she sees in front of her. She tells of how it sits, how it sings, how it moves to her from a fixed and singular viewpoint. She searches for words to approximate colours, textures, materials, processes that would have been used to work it into being. She's careful. She tests them out piece by piece into her microphone and grips on to the most fitting. Always feeling the gap between the thing that comes into her eyes and the thing that comes out of her mouth, The Surgeon tries hard to stick with the It up close, to hear it properly and understand its demands. Having exhausted this first attempt at verbal portraiture she pauses, waits to know whether a response will come.

There's an empty delay. No reply.

Time passes and nothing comes back.

After accepting that her voice has reverberated onward and met no ground or mass, The Surgeon calls out again, tries to tell The Dancer what she sees in the dark. Her long attempts at translating the solid thing in front of her pour out of her mouth and drip through the tiny holes of her microphone. They're certainly going somewhere.

Attempting to hunt down the problem, The Surgeon follows the trail of speech back into her body. She listens to the words as they form in her head, get moulded in her mouth, flush out of her. By the time she's observed them reaching her ears it's clear where at least one of the issues is; her words are coming out of her unfinished, missing corners and clarity and precision.

> *I'm noticing how the earlier joy has deflated out of The Surgeon's body, the weight of her head rounding her shoulders.*

The Surgeon thinks back to the speed with which she both made the decision to cut off her tongue and then moved her scalpel and acted upon it. She wiggles the nub that remains at the back of her oral cavity and glances at the flaccid lump she cast aside that once rolled and lapped as a boneless limb. With this new version of her body, it's easier to absorb but harder to transmit. The path from brain to outside world has been severed. She'll have to find another way.

Taking her hand out from the mug that The Surgeon only now remembers has been containing her fist for this past amount of time, she picks up her dismembered tongue. Examining the fleshy appendage, so recently added to the world, she picks off the stray fluff that's stuck to its moistness and brings it close to her chest to be illuminated in the harshness of the screen. Holding it pincer-grip between thumb and forefinger, she rotates it, logging individual taste buds and their jobs in this world.

I'm investigating with her in the minutiae of the taste bud landscape, but feeling like I'm about to be yanked somewhere else, darting around like a stickleback. I'm struggling not to think about things that have nothing to do with It (from a cave); project plans, confusions, to-do lists, kids. I'm trying to come back.

Another body memory suddenly swallows The Surgeon; she is a child of around ten, and she's plucked an ice lolly from the freezer, rocket shaped, a near mirror to the empty hollow of her own mouth. She's stuck the lolly in her mouth, sucked tight to the frozen-dry chunk. As she pulls it out ready for another go, a new layer of sensation fills her. It sits on top of the layers of cold and flavour and smothers them almost entirely. Pain layer. Having to pull hard on the wooden stick and investigating at speed, she sees huddled on the surface of the ice a cluster of pinkish taste buds, ripped from their roots, decapitated and now dying. That the treat could stick to her young body so coldly that it would rip out a piece rather than give in to being melted. She feels again the childish surprise at how easily the human body can be altered; a thought that she carries with her into theatre every shift.

So it's not the first time that The Surgeon has pulled off a piece of this organ. Coming round from this latest episode of time travel with tongue still in fingers, she presses its surface once more onto her laptop screen. This time she presses it hard, doesn't move it around. She isn't interested in tasting the flat façade but instead wants it to suck up the picture underneath it. She wills it deep within, hopes that it can bring to her its knowledge from the image realm.

Without fanfare, The Surgeon's tongue melts through the display in front of her and is sucked into the deep blackness ahead, leaving her grasping onto emptiness.

I'm watching now from within the dark repository as the section of tongue slaps to the ground aside The Dancer. I'm hearing that the floor here does exist, and is hard, at least fairly smooth, probably dry.

With this abrupt entrance, it's clear that the scaling has gone awry in this enclave of the archive. A boundless black space, with It (from a cave) in the middle and a tongue on the floor beside it, but the units of measurement that were embedded in this It have been pulled out of sync during the object–image translation. Proportionally to the artefact, and to the segments of The Dancer that came in and out of the picture, the piece of The Surgeon's tongue that has landed beside them is colossal. It waits, unmoving, like a dozing sea lion or a beached manatee. The Surgeon lifts her palm towards the screen to shield herself from the horror of her own body turned beastly, and as she does so, unintentionally measures the length of her forefinger up against this new monster. The image of it is still life-sized. It matches up with the size of her life now, out here, at 1:1 ratio. There must be a hole in the formatting.

The Surgeon ponders the proximity of the piece of herself to the mass of The Dancer and to the body of the It. She's getting closer to them. The Surgeon hopes she can find a way closer still.

Sweaty
juices catalysing
sticky stinks. Acrid vinegars.
Transformation of acidic to metallic
to the coppery taste as a kid sneaking
a lick of a hot, old penny cooking on the
dashboard that's been circulating through
pockets and across palms.
All recorded in the deep depth of the unglossiness.
Lack, or gain, of sheen and lustre. Round token.
Point of exchange, unit of trade, declaration of
something. Flatness. But with critical surface ridges
for agreeing contracts, performing talismanic duties.
Sturdy droplet, smashed out by forcing steely genes
into an empty, cavernous mirror.
For it to become one legible and accepted circulatory
totem among many. And this particular integer
savoured above others. Clefts patterning its face,
clefts calling out as part of a chorus. Those noisy
fissures catching passing debris, recording its
journeying across place and time and puddle and
palm. Edges with extra edging, crimping and
barcoding, speaking to nails rasping along
it. Declaration of desire to meet digits
and (treasure) chests. Sonorous
and glorious and ringing.

7. It (a round one)

I'm surveying within an edgeless white, with It (a round one) hovering in mid-air ahead, and observing as The Dancer enters the space from out of the white. I'm noting that although the surface of the floor can't be identified exactly, The Dancer is traversing it perfectly well, and so something solid must exist beneath her feet.

Just floating, with no ties to a surface, It (a round one) pivots about its vertical axis, propped improbably on one of its edges. It has a flat part that looks towards the face of The Dancer, who reaches out into the whiteness and plucks it from mid-air. She does so without ceremony. The sense of anticipation that she once felt at the prospect of touching such a thing lapsed long ago.

Observing as usual from her digital perch, The Surgeon sees The Dancer pick up the small object and place it in her palm, but she can't yet make out its intricacies.

I'm feeling in The Surgeon's stomach layers of jealousy and resentment settling on top of the already heady concoction of awe and longing. A thread within the jealousy strand of her emotions is directed at the tiny creature squirming knowledge into itself from the inside of The Dancer, and with this realisation is added a sprinkling of shame. These feelings are spreading into a deep exhaustion that's settling on The Surgeon's shoulders. They're pulling on the corners of her mouth. She's been like this too long, sat here, trying. I'm watching from behind her curved spine.

With no real hope that it will engender any progress, but with no other ideas coming into mind, The Surgeon clips out a sequence over the keys. She taps out a string of letters that, maybe, will be long enough and solid enough to extend the length of the distance between the three parties involved. The Surgeon is looking, literally, for another channel through which to communicate with The Dancer and the It. She wants any way to get through and be close to them. She types into the chat, hits 'send to all panellists and participants and objects and anything else that might be listening' and sits back.

Nothing yet in response.

I'm warming up. I'm moving now in the looser space of The Dancer. I'm not being pulled around, not being hit in the face with things that happened elsewhere, or things that may or may not come to pass. I'm in it, with it.

Whether conscious of her decision to or not, The Dancer moves her body. Within the bright, surfaceless whiteness, she slightly raises her shoulder, bends her elbow, lifts forearm, twists wrist, uncurls fingers, tilts head down. The It is now directly in front of her nose, taking up almost the entirety of her field of vision with its delightful glare. With her other hand, she lifts off her short-sight-correcting glasses and places them on her head in order to see this close-up thing more clearly, removing the last unnecessary mediating layer between them. She sees the pits in its body that map out its unique constellation, its own personal fingerprint embedded into its mass-produced bones. One of so many and yet so special, so immaculate.

I'm returning to The Surgeon to feel her tensing, frustrating. She has no equivalent layer to remove and reveal to bask in.

At the lack of acknowledgement of her response, The Surgeon repeats her gestures and types again. She sends the request into the ether. She's not concerned with what the words of the message say, but that just with the presence of a block of letters she can announce that there is somebody who sent it who needs a reply.

sodijvdiuhsdcskjdc
dcijsdvjkna
acknskvnsdkldckaldcnasbckadncvkdjvbkjdvba

I'm back at The Dancer, resting stationary with her, standing in the white of the archive.

There's a kick from within. Maybe it's a limb or a club that hoofs her from the inside. A blow in the darkness that she didn't see coming and that she couldn't brace herself for. Her lower organs absorb the force that's readying itself for life outside. She hopes they can hold. Following the lead of the inner one that will soon be outside, The Dancer lifts her mind's eye out from her uterus and returns it to the external body resting in her hand. At first cold and other, the It has now warmed to sing in unison with her. It's drawn from her and is copying her condition.

Like an observer outside of the scene, The Dancer notices that her arm and her hand are moving again. She's aware of her upper back muscles tensing and her upper arm rising. She knows that she's bringing her open fist closer to her face, that her lips are parting, her lower jaw dropping and her neck extending forwards. She knows what she's doing; she can feel the decisions flowing through her limbs.

The Dancer feels the air drawing into her mouth, meeting the coating of her teeth and running over her tongue. She observes from within as the aperture of her mouth closes over the entirety of It (a round one).

I'm pinging to The Surgeon.

Observing the quickly changing situation that's unfolding in front of her and that has roused her out of her sense of futility, The Surgeon bats her keyboard keys now with more vigour. This woman she's watching, so alluring and in normal circumstances so physically skilled, is being so wreckless. She finds herself making a mental list of all the foreign objects she's extracted from bodies so far: buttons, marbles, coins, batteries, animal bones, peas, magnets, dentures, hair grips, false nails, pen lids. She sends them out into the chat one by one, warning bells trying to ring out to The Dancer. Depending on the size of the apertures and the forms travelling through them, some of these units will pass through of their own accord, will easily traverse the beefy marble run and will descend, aided by gravity and peristalsis, to return to flow around the worlds' seas as discrete beings once more. Others will not slip down and be nudged back out without assistance. These things might hook themselves terribly through something soft, or stubbornly refuse to pass through one of the bodies' many inner locks and gates, remaining firmly within until someone intervenes. Which are we dealing with?

With The Dancer.

Inside The Dancer's mouth, her tongue flips the object over. There's just enough room for it to perform a 360° rotation. The addition of the foreign object has provoked her salivary glands to go into maximum output mode, sending thick spit to pool on her tongue. Capitalising on this newfound rush of lubrication she swallows the object.

While the artefact travels downwards, The Dancer is taken back to thoughts of the new body she's growing within her, of the moulding and proving that's needed to get it finished and up to full size. It requires so much to become its own unit that can withstand the shock of being out in the air. She thinks about how she knows this body inside her, that she knows it from and with the inside of herself, directly through her bones and her muscles that nestle up against her expanding uterus, feeling squiggles from semi-formed limbs and organs moving aside to accommodate hundreds of squashy bones. She knows it through the extra water sitting around her knees, and in her hair that is no longer malting onto her pillow. She wonders how this new It that has just entered will also be felt and be known from the new vantage point of being within.

Surgeon.

Infuriated and exasperated, The Surgeon rests her chin in the crook of her hand, elbow on the operating table, and looks down at her keyboard for a sign to appear to her. No message appears, just greasy flecks of crisps that must have fluttered over her workspace some time ago. Crunchy shards have nestled themselves in between the cracks of the F, G and H. She lifts her eyeline to stare at The Dancer.

I'm travelling through The Surgeon's screen and returning to the white space, and to The Dancer.

The Dancer idles. This place has nothing much to hold her now that she's eaten the precious nugget that once resided in it. She knows that her gait doesn't have the poise it did before she was pregnant, but she paces carefully forward, allowing thoughts to come to her. Absentmindedly, she rubs her bump, then rubs some more and teases out some aching muscles in need of soothing. She feels her way across the expanding version of herself, and becomes aware of the curiosity in her fingertips, searching their way around to see whether the It has slid somewhere inside her that's still slightly accessible to her fingers feeling from the outside. Maybe It (a round one) is snaking its way under her skin, visible to the touch like a marble under rolled icing.

Finding nothing except her massive stomach and her tired regular form, The Dancer continues her stepping.

I'm wondering why The Dancer has nowhere else to be. She's always present, and in the present, in spite of the ticking timebomb strapped to her front that looks like it might burst at any moment. That clearly needs to be attended to and thought about. But she's just there, being a dancer, moving at one with the world, neatly meeting the set of Its as they appear in order.

The Dancer stops her pacing. She clasps her hands under her bump for support and to try to lift herself up with her own arms. She heaves herself into the air, momentarily lifts her fat feet off the floor, thuds back down again. The Dancer carries on making these small, heavy jumps of joy, feet coming down in a syncopated pair of thuds.

In between jumps she looks up with an ear strained to the ceiling. She can't hear It (a round one) while she jumps, so she deduces that it's not resting inside her against bone. Or at least it's not resting against bone with enough space around it to bang onto it.

Experiment over, The Dancer stops her cumbersome leaps in the whiteness as a blemish on the ground catches her eye. There is something else in here after all. Her stance wide, she stoops to investigate the new entity on the illuminated ground. It takes a moment for her to decipher its form; it's a section of severed tongue. She scoops it up, cups it in her paw.

Thing to decorate.
A thin strip of wealth with the
gentle arcs of limbs, eye sockets, manes.
Shimmying up and down, wrapping around
another form while holding tight its own taught
shape. Memories within its bones of multiple
previous lives lived before having been boiled up
and bubbled up into now. Embodied glory. Quite
pretty, somewhat attractive, certainly beautiful.
Being so beautiful as strategy for survival. Made
proud and bold with furnace power that's stored
in its cold spine. Cracked out of the death mask it
was dripped into, lapped against while it learned its
own face. Finessed with fine tools, fine fingers, fine
muscles. Secretions out of the very stuff it's made
from. Dried oozes of potent sweat announcing the
reactions between body of object and body of
outside. Replies to conversations that change the
structure of its matter. A new skin shuddered
out to solidify and meet the world, protecting
the looping strands of DNA underneath. This
outer layer crunching and scratchy under
teeth. Chalky. Ouroboros-like, but
winding out both ways; two heads
like a mythical beast, not one
head one tail like a coin.

8. It (that exists)

The Dancer knows that this thing must be particularly remarkable, because it exists. It is in front of her and able to be experienced. It's not part of the class of objects that are *supposedly lost and then supposedly found*, or the class of objects that are *touched by someone or something narratively exciting*; it's part of the class of objects that are *peer reviewed and deemed pretty good and so not for destruction at this particular moment*. Its quality is enacted through its not having been liquefied and then improved upon. It's not been assessed and considered as lacking by someone with the knowledge to understand its technical formation and aesthetic design. It's been allowed to remain. And as it remains it loops.

> *I'm encountering It (that exists) alongside The Dancer in a greyish room, inoffensive to the eyes, so as to let the single object sing out on top of the single table in this section of the repository. I'm watching from above standard head height, eyeline angled downwards to see the majority of The Dancer and the It on its waist-level surface.*

The Dancer has a banal encounter with this It, as one might meet a set of keys on the sideboard. It (that exists) is resting on a table, casting mid-tone shadows that announce its submission to gravity's influence.

Following The Dancer's recent ingestion of one of her finds, she contemplates whether eating the object would be an appropriate strategy for getting to know this thing too. Although it's a friendly enough form, it's most probably too big to go down her gullet in its current arrangement, and mangling it in order for it to become swallowable seems to her an extreme first decision.

I'm watching from the other side of the table as The Dancer gazes on.

In the antithesis of her previous manoeuvre, instead of eating this thing, of letting it reside inside her, The Dancer takes a cue from the circling thing in front of her, and envisions her body inhabiting its body, of going inside and through the object to live within it. There's a small opening, which could be a place to begin. She imagines being on the inside looking out, through its eyes. She peers into the inviting hole and assumes the pose of a diver with hands in prayer position above her head. She starts to slip the tips of her middle fingers through the gap, feels the edges of it graze her knuckles, ring dully over her protruding wrist bones. (There's no pregnancy-water retaining in that part of The Dancer, her frame still feels sharp and exposed.)

I'm noticing that The Surgeon is here again too, watching and willing from a place beyond reach. I'm hearing the artificial lens release of screen-grabs as she tries to keep The Dancer still in her bounding box, tickling the pixels of her extremities. Swiping also to catch portraits of the It.

With little shimmies The Dancer encourages It (that exists) past her pair of elbows, but the aperture is getting tighter around her increasingly obtuse form. Shifting her shoulder blades and collarbones, she wills herself deeper into the object and edges its mouth further up her arms. Shifting and inching onwards, her own body is still arranged with palms together, arms stretched overhead, so that the usually clear space between her upper arms now contains her own head-encased brain.

Her biceps are pinning her ears flat to the sides of her skull, noises of her internal workings amplified inside her concealed eardrums. The Dancer's head goes forth and the bulk of her presses her body further into the object on the table. When the opening of the object meets The Dancer at her widest part – the crest of her shoulders – the attempt begins to stall. She pictures the bodies of world record attempts for the fastest fit through a toilet seat; recalls wrestles in dance class changing rooms with crystal encrusted Lycra: be a body that's long and sparse and stringy.

I'm seeing these skittish body references as The Dancer rebuilds them in her mind, channelling old shapes and old knowledge.

I'm feeling, too, the restlessness in The Surgeon's hips, as she's stuck, unable to add the pressure that can grab on and be a force to act against. The things she would do if she were there too.

The Dancer doesn't currently possess either of the bodies writhing in her mind's eye, but she lives through the images to power her way further into the thing. Straining against herself, she forces onwards and It (that exists) at last clears the ridge of her left shoulder.

And then it's gone.

Breathless with effort and relief, The Dancer is back at the edge of the table that the thing is no longer sat on. Where the object lay is now just an empty surface. She leans forward to inspect more closely what isn't there, and in doing so is startled by something frightening leaping out from under her armpits.

Watery thin and yet with the gleam of a blade, something flashes into being and vanishes just as momentarily. The Dancer gracefully repeats the sway of her top half in an attempt to reproduce the mirage. An image slice reappears, then swiftly retreats, and then partially reappears with a flash as she tilts again. It wails out, and then goes to nothing, keeping time with her sweeping gestures. At one moment stillness, and then a flicker that's merged into her own silhouette. She's managed to step inside a version of this thing, has worked herself underneath its render. Her body is now entwined inside something that was previously other, has worked her way so close to the edge of the object that she can see the mesh malfunctioning up close. She's inhabiting the boundary of this It.

I'm watching as a slice of an image rears out of The Dancer's chest like a hologram and is promptly sucked back into invisibility. I'm feeling her pleasure as I watch her play with the anomaly within her.

The Dancer beams the object out of her chest and sees it slip back in. She's a woman who learns her world through the stuff she finds as she scrabbles around in the dirt: as the points on her body meet the facets of others, as she absorbs their voices of materiality and form and texture and weight. Things that are direct and honest and knowable if they are listened to attentively enough.

The Dancer's mind is drawn now, as it increasingly is, to the bump that's edging further out in front of her. It feels somewhat thing-like to her at this moment, safely contained and swimming like a pickle in a jar, but how to know it (them!) when they're squiggling about in the world with agency of their own?

With her unthinking mind forging on and directing her limbs, and her consciousness lagging behind, piecing the moves together after, The Dancer pulls the piece of tongue out from the fold she stashed it in. She practices positioning her arms to make a cradle and strokes a soothing finger down its side, searching for a trace of human warmth within.

The Dancer imagines what it might be like to hold her own baby. She thinks hopefully about being bonded with something so tightly that it's impossible to turn away from it.

> *I'm flicking through The Dancer's mental images of all-consuming togetherness as the weight of the mass in her arms makes itself known to her muscles. And I'm feeling pictures of being parted: hands being let go of and new things being picked up in their place, new scenes being built without The Dancer centre stage.*

Even before this new person has been born, The Dancer can feel the undercurrent of devastation that's sunk across the base of her love for them.

The daydream marches straight through her feeling of easiness and the fun that she found so recently in playing her body around a small, looping object.

Adjusting her arms and trying to bring herself back to something sort-of tangible, The Dancer tries to dab The Surgeon's severed tongue onto the thing that is half trapped and half liberated under her armpits. With her swaying and its flashing, she tries to get the two forms to meet, tests whether the disembodied taste buds can find the thing she can't quite make out.

I'm switching back to The Surgeon, soaking up the shock as it ripples down her face, forcing her eyes to widen, head to sink back, mouth to gape.

The Surgeon feels sections of her brain light up. She can feel something coming through, there's knowledge entering inside of her. This is a new kind of knowing in her body, and one that makes no logical sense, which certainly goes against what she was taught at medical school but is undeniably now sitting concretely within her.

She struggles to find accurate vocabulary to process the occurrence. The flavour isn't yet whole and legible for her, but the truth that there has been a conversation between The Dancer's body and her own shakes The Surgeon into a new present. She's tasted something of this thing, she's been able to absorb a facet of its form through her own bumpy skin.

There's been a relay of sorts. An event from within the archive has made it out and into The Surgeon's head. It's not necessary to be translated through some other means; it jumped right in while she wasn't trying. She wants more.

Unable to send anything out for The Dancer to register and hungry for tastes, The Surgeon silently wills The Dancer to rub her tongue over more things. The Dancer continues her slow wriggles, making movements so the flash reveals itself, then swaying to collide it into the tongue.

I'm remembering through The Dancer the knee action of peeling off wet leggings.

After one of her sways to the side, the thing that's stuck around and through The Dancer's chest stops appearing. Her movements have given the object a final shove, and now It (that exists) has been dislodged and is vanished.

It hasn't fallen back out of her and reappeared on the tabletop; she's lost it. A stream of labels describing the action that might have taken place fall metaphorically onto The Surgeon:

Lost
Disappeared
Vanished
Melted
Transformed
Enveloped
Broken
Hidden
Recycled
Destroyed

All of which seem to her improbable if not wholly impossible. That the particles that comprise this It have been annihilated, totally transformed or made invisible. Been hidden or melted, broken or transformed, lost or vanished.

As this losing unfolds, there's another critical event. Although arguably her hands are her most important tool for cutting into and rebuilding bodies, in The Surgeon's mind it's her laptop that holds the most powerful position in her arsenal. It's the endlessly nesting folders of ever-visible data that make it feel important, rather than the truly countless manoeuvres and hours of flight time that her hands have clocked up quietly within them.

And today the laptop malfunctions.

In her theatre, watching The Dancer, rejoicing at the possibility of tasting the world, gritting teeth at the stuckness of the rest of her, the barely audible radio plays through the tinny speakers of The Surgeon's laptop. It provides the usual chattering backdrop to her day of work and leisure. And now it cuts out. Wiggling a finger on the trackpad does nothing to awaken the black screen. Holding the power button doesn't resuscitate it either. She smells something singed. It's not deep like the smell of cauterising flesh, yet there's a bloody, metallic note that's not unfamiliar to her.

A whirlpool of bereavement cycles through her guts. With knowing foolishness, she begins to tally the extent of the loss; hard-won final pdfs, phone photo backups, wordcounts, screengrabs of the It and The Dancer. She stops herself before it becomes too massive to think about. How could she be so stupid.

This part of the archive is deteriorating. The Surgeon's portal onto it, the Its and The Dancer, is now closed. She has no means of communicating. She thinks about the unannounced fracturing of her prized device, wonders what will give way next. Whether The Dancer is trapped inside, paradoxically alone inside the museum with the unborn one. It's too much.

With keratin
power of animal claw, scale, fur.
Shielding and transporting
things in front to and from
things behind. Crux to lean
on and be absorbed
by so that there's
no need to be
constrained by one's
own temperament or the way one
usually meets the world. Teaching lessons
on concealment, how to be another, how to
travel through, move beyond to somewhere
embodied. Armoured plate with gaps between
for glimpsing inside. Armoured plate with gaps
in between for peeking out. Channelling strength
structures that borrow forces from nature, that have
grown cell by cell, metamorphosed sugar into
tooth. With protrusion-ruptured horns to dowse
for friend and foe. Ritualistic sniffing out of
living and dead. Movements flow through
the circuitous tunnels of this thing made
to let dances fall out of a body.
Becoming puppet, becoming puppet-
master. Bony death mask façade
mimicking surface topography.
Fierce emotion glued tight, first
impression always identical.

9. It (a performance)

After sweating hours or minutes in front of the inanimate metal hinge, The Surgeon has encouraged her laptop to regain consciousness. It's blinked on and is limping along in *safe mode*, able only to output in limited colours, sounds and operations. She hopes that the *safe mode* can stretch to offering some protection to The Dancer too.

> *I'm being with both The Surgeon and The Dancer in their separate spaces; The Surgeon seated as always, same room, laptop ahead, portal on screen open into museum but not as detailed or smooth as before; The Dancer in the vault of the next It moving around a creamy room.*

The Surgeon meets It (a performance) as an object that is also a facet of The Dancer herself.

The Surgeon's screen has The Dancer positioned at its centre. The Dancer is moving her arms, legs, head, bump, in repeating loops; she's dancing. Not any recognised set of moves that would have a name, but a dance of unthinking flows of rhythms. It (a performance) is dancing too; they've merged. The Surgeon looks for hints to explain to her whether The Dancer has been taken over by the It, if she is the articulator of its moves and the driving force of its body; or if it's the other way around and she has taken it over and is forcing its angles and crevices to move to her beat. It's possible that they're tangoing like a murmuration of starlings, reading each other and acting with imperceptible agility. Whatever it is, they move as one.

Stolen. Appropriated. In urgent need of repatriation.

I'm feeling concern and wariness in The Surgeon's eyelids and firmly closed lips.

Observing, The Surgeon isn't sure what to make of what she sees in front of her. Or rather she knows what she feels about the situation but doesn't know what to do about it to make it any better. She should probably turn it off, look away, write someone a letter.

I'm remaking an image of The Surgeon as a teenager, with fine plaits all over her head exposing her white scalp between thin, brown twists. I'm watching the wrapping in bright wool to make it seem more exciting. To bring in some colour. Bring in some culture.

This It isn't for playing with. It has meaning and complexity and difficulty that The Dancer isn't entitled to dance over. The Surgeon wants to do something about it, finds herself tapping an angry knuckle on her screen as if trying to shoo a cat off a carrot patch.

The Dancer stops dancing and turns to look directly at The Surgeon. Movements slowed by surprise, The Surgeon cautiously taps a nail, clicking it back at her against the plastic. The Dancer holds her gaze and covers her ears with her hands, frowning.

I'm pinning into place by the direct boring of The Dancer's eyes.

This would be considered progress, but The Surgeon's desperation for closeness is becoming unbearable.

She yearns for proper contact, for squashy bodies and pressing and no more dry, clicking buttons. She feels that she's stuck on the outside, removed from the space of real action. She's being held at the textbook learning stage, not allowed to progress to working with real patients, surrounded by stand-ins instead. She wants to be down there with The Dancer, not an ape behind Perspex. The joy at having made contact with the woman she has been longing for is underpinned by a deep sadness in her stomach.

The Surgeon holds her hand steady where she left it on her screen, energy faded by lowness.

Another radical move is needed to counter it.

The Surgeon grips on to the black outer edge of her laptop screen and pulls her head closer to it, so that she can smell the pulsing charge and feel the warm electrical glow on her lips. She continues leaning forward, pushing her forehead to meet the screen's edge. She forces on, head butted against the glass, playing with the shift of her skull under the give in her skin as it sticks her in place. She pushes harder still, trying to impose a way through, and feels a give in her temporal lobe, an enveloping and sinking into the abyss of her screen. Her face vanishing beyond the glass plane, The Surgeon moves her head through the open porthole to inhabit the unchartered depths beyond. Hands pulling shoulders through and torso following, knees clambering onto keypad, she climbs through the newly created trapdoor, scrabbling the whole of her body into the inside and out of the other. She's delighted at the prospect of some change, finally; a hint of getting nearer to being able to touch and rub and fondle something real. To butt up against and nestle down on a thing.

I'm floating in an indescribable position that has no image in my mind's eye. It's a sensation I can't find words to stand in for.

A distant and nostalgic flavour is hitting The Surgeon. It's too hazy to place immediately, and too fleeting to analyse logically, but nevertheless it landed somewhere. It was a taste that came to her not through taste buds and smell receptors but through memory. And now it's passed.

A bird flies by.

Her teeth feel weird. The fact that The Surgeon's aware of feeling them is a warning bell. She realises it's been ages since she went to the dentist. Her mouth feels too small. It doesn't usually act like a cavity; it's normally clamped shut and full of tongue that's flicking away at the gaps between her lower incisors. Except not now, it's just a vague bit of her body, its function dubious.

The Surgeon comes to from these passing observations with the horizon line running vertically down her field of vision. She notes pressure points at her ankle bone, knee, hip, shoulder, head, where one side of her is meeting something cold and unyielding. As she makes an attempt at rearranging herself, she realises she's on the floor, lying down in a shape that resembles the recovery position. This is lucky, because as she moves she feels the inner knowledge of recent blunt trauma in both her knees, elbows and jawbone. She wonders if The Dancer is nearby and able to offer some soothing. She lays where she is a little longer and allows her eyes to close.

Slick,
slippery, wet, singing.
Quiet dynamism ringing out from
behind ballooning walls. Visible hollows
bubbled into life inside wall-enclosed cavities.
Bubbled into compartments, trapped gases
of old, old breath, flowing wisps of places it
sat in. Eked out of leaking sand, dripping in
geological time. An object to look through, as
a filter applicable to landscapes beyond it,
reflecting new hazes of light, shifting tone
in the distance. Constellation of pockets
congealed in specific anthropomorphic
arrangement, like a twisting modelled
balloon poodle, suggestive, not
anatomically accurate, evoking
cartoonish beastly bovine.
Humped, harnessed entity, with
neat edges, features drawn in
efficiently defined globules.
Lollipop wetness, hard-crack
transparency. Invitation for
licking, surfaces voicing smooth,
frictionless, speaking velocity,
viscosity. Fragility as hard
shell. Lacquered badge declaring
delicate brittleness of bloated body.
One tap deliciously sonorous, one more
likely total smashing devastation.

10. It (semi-transparent)

When The Surgeon regains consciousness a second time, she takes in the enormity of what has happened. She's entered into the archive. Finally, she's made it beyond the boundary and has entered herself as a new solid thing into object space. She's got the chance to get her body right up inside something, to roll around in the joy of the actual world.

> *I'm flitting between observing The Surgeon lying motionless on the floor and seeing the edge of the ground that she's lying on from out of her eyeballs, with It (semi-transparent) straight ahead.*

The Surgeon brings herself to standing inside the black chasm of her surroundings. It's so black as to have no visible surfaces except for a patch of floor made known by a small pool of light holding It (semi-transparent).

On the opposite edge of the pool of light The Dancer comes into being.

> *I'm retreating to take in the entireties of both women and of It (semi-transparent) basking in its personal spotlight.*

The Dancer and The Surgeon are for the first time occupying the same cuboid of space and air. Each one of them is exhaling particles that the other one then sucks in, motes of dust taking it in turns to cycle through the two pairs of lungs. Such a delicate act of penetration.

Desperate to connect, The Surgeon extends her arm over the object sitting between them and feels a zing as her fingertip meets The Dancer. The warmth of the response in her finger cascades throughout her whole being. It's powerful, being able to touch, being so close so as to meet with just a lean or a reach, without even having to move a foot.

The Surgeon reaches out again to make a touch, to feel again the wonder of merging another body with her own. The Dancer smiles, pleased by the wordless conversation unfolding between them. This second time, the magic The Surgeon feels is a little smaller than the first, and she goes in for a harder third squeeze in an attempt to find a touch that will knock her over like the first did.

The Dancer laughs at the force of this latest move and retaliates with a nudge to The Surgeon's left side. The Surgeon hadn't anticipated what it would feel like to be touched back like that, to provide the corresponding cushion to The Dancer's delicate arm. She liked it.

They continue in this way, batting each other's limbs off one another, playing a rally of nudges and shoves with It (semi-transparent) an obedient puppy at their feet. First, an adjustment of a foot to centre a leg gone off balance, and then a wilful shuffle forwards to be able to reach more of the other human being in front. After barely a moment the shunts turn to grabs and within a few breaths they're holding each other, hugging tightly with suffocating love. The Surgeon and The Dancer hustle and grasp, consuming as much of the other as the practicalities of their bodies will allow, hands inching further around backs, chins nuzzling deeper into necks.

I'm feeling the longing now. To be there too.
To know the joy of pressing and being pressed.

The Surgeon and The Dancer settle to hold the embrace, singing the exhale to the other's inhale, locked in a coil of tessellating bodies, two fully grown ones, one still on its way.

Breaths slowing down, joined in this moment, the thoughts of the two women mingle. In their minds they ask one another about what it is to become one solid thing, to merge, to become totally still, to stop. How it might feel to become static together, like the thing that rests on the floor between them. They pick out memories as case studies to feel what could be possible: of calcified stones removed from near quivering tonsils; of centuries-old stained glass slumped into pools at the bottom of lead frames; of polished floor tiles holding slices of ammonites captured mid-breath; of the marble balustrades of the Sacré-Coeur worn into curves by kids trying to get a better view. Everywhere they look they find things not totally hard and solid, but things living fallibly and unpredictably; growing and morphing and breathing and shifting.

Together they feel a heightened sense of protectiveness over this latest object they're meeting. That although it's been cushioned safely within the pomp of the object repository, this thing, like everything else, is at the whim of the universe, is just as solid as a meringue in a tornado.

From inside the museum, and having been prickled by another's touch, The Surgeon's body acts and knows differently. She's about to use it to hold her first enthralling and magnificent It. The Surgeon takes a breath, reaches down to pick It (semi-transparent) up, and tucks it under her arm for safekeeping. As if the adoration of her fleshy wing could offer the object something that material and taxonomic protections alone could not.

Sad jigsaw. Not built as a puzzle, not intended in the phase of its imagining to be bits, pieces, so many edges butted up. Once one single unit, now plural individuals settled up against each other, edge facing edge, choreographed on front of a landscape. The majority is missing, a map of missing gaps. Main mother island holds the middle, with offspring pieces clustered next, and outer shores cleverly filled with pretend, scallop-edged chunks tessellating to follow broken bones. Not new bits looking exactly like old pieces to be fully illusory; not new bits looking brand new to stick out too hard; instead, bland middle medium: polite in between just surrounding, sitting tamely in place. Bevelled mantlepieces that are still not it, leading onto section that is it with dusty decorative brail – ravines, arches, kernels – speaking patches of glorious, bucolic monotone. Scene sliced vertical, sprig-moulded on top of same, hinting at wealthy climes. Hard-leaved skeletons reclining amid dry lusciousness.

11. It (in pieces)

I'm scanning a room lit by daylight, with windows, brickwork, plug sockets, fire extinguisher taking their places on the walls of this part of the museum alongside It (in pieces). Hand in hand, The Surgeon and The Dancer are strolling through, The Dancer relishing having another body bodying alongside her, and The Surgeon glad to have a mercurial lead to follow. I'm seeing them come to a stop in front of the next It.

Standing in front of It (in pieces), The Surgeon is thinking about death. It's common in her profession but has been brought to the fore more strongly and more personally following the recent act of love between her and The Dancer, and on witnessing the decrepit state of the thing in her current eyeline.

If The Dancer, potential receptacle of her love, was cremated right now, what would remain? The Surgeon pictures the wooden box containing the ashes of a friend paraded in front of mourners, bigger than the usual unit of dust not because he was a particularly big friend, but because he had a titanium knee that withstood the furnace flames. She wanted so much to see what his knee looked like after, how it had been changed by the heat. But that wouldn't have been polite. He was not that close a friend. Nothing of The Dancer would likely get left behind in this way, rather, as would befit someone with her occupation, she would become entirely airborne, perhaps leaving It (a round one) and It (that exists) to find a way back out of her insides to move around, charred, back into circulation.

I'm watching them both looking at the It. They're concentrating primarily on the jumbling daydreams inside their heads but they're attempting to appear attentive to the object before them.

The Surgeon is fixating on her vulnerability to outside forces, and is lost in a soup of thoughts about custom foam packing inserts, and pacemakers, and bum fillers, and golden sheet masks, and staying young, and delaying the inevitable, and keeping things for special occasions, and living to the fullest, and looking after things, and being open to love, and being careful, and getting rid of stuff.

The Surgeon pictures her set of felt pens, the black one still missing. It's understandable to feel frustration when possessions go astray, but for The Surgeon it's always an immense boulder of a problem when she can't locate even the most insignificant of things. The black out of a set of felt pens, a phone case that is definitely in her theatre but also still lost, a coat that really suited her, some beads she bought on a holiday. Losing things for The Surgeon results in a shift in the background of all following events until the item is either found again or replaced with an exact match or by something superior. It means an upturning and emptying multiple times, of revisiting steps, of shunting the to-do list to make way for the pernickety searching that takes priority. Phone case located (sort of) logically in a drawer of electrical things. Coat gone forever but replaced by an identical second-hand one found online. The black pen, most recent loss, is still sitting high up on her list of jobs, occupying what she feels is the top-right corner of her brain. With these minor losses felt in her heart so intently, the mass of proper, big losses still yet to have happened – of her entire youth, her health and faculties, and of love and The Dancer herself – inhabit the form of a wall so impenetrable that The Surgeon cannot even face its sheer edge.

> *I'm drawing a squeezing of hands, sketching the swallowing of a lump in a throat.*

A mirror to the body but with none of its flesh. No muscle and pulsing, just a clumsy skeleton without organs, squiggles, gestures. All right-angled bones and jointless corners standing firm without nuance. An efficient collection of lines meeting lines, holding each other in place, holding apart, describing the spaces in between and around. Juts butt in, cut across, rest on for support. Propping lengths of pick-up sticks with planar sheets slicing through and inserting dimensions. A knocking noise, hollow, organic. Charred xylophone lengths contrast bright school tones accenting axis and edge. Gloss over the skin on its many limbs, appearing to hold briefly in arrangement, not matt or silk but wipe-clean, oil-based. Tepee for prostrating over; chunky, solid hammock suggesting semblance of rest.

12. It (mirror-like)

With The Surgeon's developing closeness with objects, the growing safety of The Dancer's love, and the new knowledge she has discovered within her own body, what she sees as the next logical step is to meld herself fully with something, keep it safe inside her.

I'm spying them both from the front edge of
a bare room; the next pocket in the taxonomy.
I'm watching The Surgeon surveying the single
It presented within the otherwise empty space.

The Dancer hangs back to allow The Surgeon the space to act out her recently uncovered agency on the abrupt and angular thing that awaits.

The scale of It (mirror-like) is different to the other objects that each of the pair have encountered so far. The object pokes its extremities out into a wider space, holds a similar unit of space to The Surgeon herself, and commands a similar request for an introduction. She notices how its structure is not so dissimilar from her own, and that as a basic understanding of anatomy can be applicable from one mammal to another, her ability to read bones and joints puts her in a good position to understand this being too.

And then she catches herself, realises that she's going about it wrong. The Surgeon is thinking with her brain again, and not her ancient body brain. Rather than pasting logic onto this It from afar, The Surgeon makes a move. She goes over to It (mirror-like) and, batting away internal voices telling her she's doing something bad, folds herself onto it, adjusting herself to best match its posture and reach. She takes herself through an introductory meditation, feels the points where her body meets something other. She notes elbows on hard solid bar, wrists draping over an edge, the right-angle digging into her flimsy, veiny flesh. The sensory vagueness of her buttock flesh is meeting something hard, smooth, flat. She feels an edge jut into the soft back of her knees, not painfully so but present enough for her to register, and another meeting of her calves against cool flatness.

In order to meet this object as fully as she can, The Surgeon has assumed an awkward stretching stance, with her arms and legs perpendicular but her pelvis sunk, her hips overreaching outwards, and her torso launching backwards so that her gaze is aimed at the join where the wall meets the ceiling. This is a position purely for looking inwards and conversing with the object, and not at all for meeting the eye of any person or other thing at ground level.

> *I'm logging the awkward repose of The Surgeon plastered over the top of It (mirror-like). I'm feeling her discomfort through her straining neck tendons and the clenching of the stub of her tongue. I'm asking myself if she actually has got better at this after all.*

The Dancer has tiptoed off into the middle distance, hands supporting the dip in her lower back, and The Surgeon is all-consumed by her task of merging. The Surgeon sinks down into her mapping, concentrating on the points where she meets the It. The actions remind her of a particular guided meditation she used to do, involving picturing oneself as an ice cube in the sun, gradually melting away and evaporating into the air. She'd worked through the process a handful of times, using the teacher's voice to help her shut off from the speed of theatre by dutifully projecting into her mind's eye the image of a cuboid of ice, inhabited by her being. During one iteration of the meditation, the vocabulary of the guidance from her teacher shifted, and left her stranded. Rather than the usual suggestion to picture yourself as an ice cube, for one rotation the words she received were to picture yourself as a *human-shaped* ice cube. Had she been doing it wrong? Each time she did this meditation, The Surgeon had been transposing her figure into a cuboid of frozen water, like a caterpillar breaking down its body to metamorphose in the cocoon, rather than just freezing her own shape so as to be able to melt it into calmness.

> *I'm coming back to the join between wall*
> *and ceiling by an alarm ringing from behind*
> *The Surgeon's knee.*

Although she's embarrassed at her misunderstanding, The Surgeon brushes it off and decides that the meditative analogy for melting is just the tool she needs. She leans back, settles down, eyes closed, brings her awareness onto her heart centre, onto the breath. Her mind's eye drifts around her insides, clocking the points she listed earlier, mapping the meeting points of the surfaces of these two beings.

The Surgeon allows herself to sink down further onto the It. Into it. Boundaries announcing the edges of person and thing, and the lines separating one thing from another, slowly start to fuzz over. Gradually, the pressing edges of her limbs against the pressed limbs of the object enmesh, like flour passing through a sieve, and The Surgeon's body drops down, coming to rest inside It (mirror-like).

Encapsulated.

She's done it. She is knowing this thing now with her whole being. It's lodged deep within, safely logged in the centre of her, and she can liberate it from its empty room, take it with her and articulate it.

The Surgeon feels the insides of the object as she does her own bones and organs. It creaks in and out with her breath and speaks with the movements of her arms and legs. The Surgeon practices moving the newly merged bodies around the room, eyeing The Dancer for reassurance as she tries out shapes and forms. Enjoying The Surgeon's newfound ability to produce phrases and expressions, The Dancer joins them on the floor, making small movements in between the object-body with her own, being pleased by moves that she would have thought ugly before her body shifted to house the growing baby.

The two women and their collection of other pieces – babies and Its and hair bobbles – take their time dancing together in silence, with just the noises of feet meeting floor, fabric brushing fabric, and breath circulating bodies to accompany them. Settling into rhythms and actions, the dancing filling the entire stage of their focus for these moments, The Surgeon and The Dancer are lifted out from the bounds of the museum, to a place of feeling and sensation and the certain knowledge of one another. A bonding ritual, an upping of XP. Love growing between them.

I'm logging the walls disintegrating into clearness, the ceiling that was resting on top floating away. A big white space remaining, with nothing else to speak of except the two, plus extras.

*And I'm returning to the original floor-wall-
ceiling-edged space. A standing still with palms
pressed on thighs to share the weight is bringing
The Dancer out of the conversation.*

With this physical thought of her baby-body,
The Dancer realises the extent of her discomfort.
Her feet, pelvis, back, head, hurt. She's tired.
    Not long to go now.

Multiple
parts from
same basic
substrate;
creamy mass
rippling throughout,
curdled into discrete
organs laid out across a
stage. Pauses between
each, celebrating parts
no longer held captive.

Sturdy base stretching out a
line, elevating portions towards
eyeballs, away from boots and
hoofs. Chunks of stage tethered
together, modular to be cheaper,
easier to move than single, long arm.

On top of long arm rests It proper; amputations
and amputees stranded lengthways. Liberated limbs,
frozen mid-play, those with lost lower lumps tethered
atop polished spikes.

Polished spikes clearly other, not for prolonged
visitor attention. Each excusing itself but
holding strong, poles for slinking around,
slipping over to meet prized masses.

Each prized mass discovered floating
within solid, allowed to reveal itself
slowly from underneath dry dust,
caressed out in whispers until
outer edge meets air.

13. It (the same)

I'm looking at The Dancer. I'm seeing her with It (unrigid) draped across her shoulders. I know that It (a round one) is homed somewhere inside her. I'm seeing a scuff on her knuckles from her run-in with It (with a face). I'm seeing the dents in her skin from journeying into It (that exists). I know that there are marks and imprints made by It (from a grave), It (a performance), and the rest, and feelings and ideas etched into her from each of these meetings that cannot be undone, can't be extracted.

I'm looking at The Surgeon. I'm seeing her with It (semi-transparent) tucked under her arm, which is now both her arm and that of It (mirror-like). I'm seeing that the finger at the end of that arm doesn't have a chunk cut out of it from a meeting with It (missing a bit), but that it felt like it should have.

I'm seeing this latest It too. It (the same) is in pieces strewn across this place. Its multiple parts and shards and slivers and chunks.

I'm seeing daytime entering as a main protagonist in this scene, and the windows with frames that permit it to do so.

In contrast to the fresh brightness of the surroundings, there's lethargy from their recent exertions overlaid onto The Dancer and The Surgeon. Their previous dance, and the much larger dance they are performing, are taking their toll. The Dancer and

The Surgeon move slowly around, switching between the rigid pieces of It (the same), dragging their splayed hands over the edges of the objects.

The Surgeon perches on the edge of one of the flatter pieces of It (the same) and places It (semi-transparent) down on the floor beside her feet in order to take off her shoes. Side by side, the It and her trainer aren't so different, but the warm smell reminds her that she's had the chance to let one of them etch itself into her gait, while the other has barely been allowed to imprint itself in her fingertips. She moves a small section of It (the same) to join the line-up on the floor, so that she can take it in alongside the others. She feels it singing in its own perfect tone, harmonising with the objects nearby.

Without speaking, The Surgeon asks The Dancer if she can help her take off It (unrigid), which has been stuck across her back all this time, to let it join the new set of classless things too. While rolling it loosely into a loaf shape, The Surgeon comes across her old tongue folded inside, cold and drying out now, and sits the two things alongside one another on the end of the row.

The Dancer wants to add something to their new subset within the archive too. She takes off her pants – she won't be able to keep them on much longer anyway – and tosses them into the pile. She picks up a Victorian woodblock print of some grapes and a drawing of vegetation from the top of a nearby plan chest, screws them into balls and throws them over onto the stack. She lets The Surgeon bear the brunt of carrying the bigger pieces of the It, and watches as the heap expands out of itself.

As they're filtering through the objects that they find in this corner of the archive, opening boxes and drawers, peeling back curtains and protective sheets, The Surgeon and The Dancer filter the things that come before them. The stuffs and lumps and volumes and masses get put in the big pile of everything that's taking up space, holding its own, speaking with myriad voices of materials and processes and makers and physicality; and all the other stuff – the facts, the labels, the scribbles, the padding – gets discarded into a jumble that has no way of being used when not sat in relation to anything in particular. These are things that have no agency in themselves, that are just lost pointers.

The taxonomy is no longer relevant, it doesn't speak to their bones like the things in themselves. Everything meeting The Surgeon and The Dancer is wonderful and singing and special, and, however lightly, leaves an impression on them.

I'm tallying this swelling set of goods as it mushrooms up and across in the sunlight.

As the mound grows, and the metadata is slowly removed, there's a cracking noise from somewhere deep within. The walls of the archive can't withstand this kind of restructuring; without the supportive information there's nothing to stop one thing from spilling over onto the next.

In her giddiness at this act of creation, The Surgeon decides that she wants to make something beautiful. She thinks about her days of cutting out tiny, useless pieces, picking up banal lengths of thread to hold worn out fasciae together. About the ugly screws and plates she hides inside. She yearns instead to make something sublime, something that will make people stop and intake a breath, that can be pilgrimaged to and worshipped. But while she's here in the archive, this rearranging and piling will have to do.

After surveying her creation from its base, The Surgeon starts a scramble up the pile. She feels the hollows and pops as pieces crack under her one shoed foot. Under the other she reads the way she is accepted and repelled by various lumps: another wild creature joining the party of stuff. Atop the collection of things, The Surgeon joins their new archive of one big load, everything made of the same, everything worthy and glorious.

Now to get The Dancer up there with her.

Lump.
Lumpy lump.
Lumpy lump offering
up glossy petrified pool.
Lumpy lump presenting glassy
spectral icing. Lumpy lump giving
glistening shifty glaze.

Weight and brutishness. A proud thing stands its ground, faces head on, squares up. Affixed to its face, something silky takes over, drags away from the usual story of big hard unit and pulls into glittering rainbow magic. Or in reverse: surface delight smacks first and holds eyeballs tight before permission to understand the hulk and heft behind is gradually revealed. Veined prisms in holographic creams. Full gamut of tonal rays.

Ushered into solid, eked out over millennia. Searched for, hunted down. Scavenged and toiled as if it was previously lost and therefore able to be once again located, except without any certainty of it ever having been laid somewhere, having definitely been pinged unhurriedly into being. Like an oyster blinking out a pearl, slow and mundane made manifest, with by-product of sheer, enticing beauty sat surprisingly on top.

14. It (lumpy)

It's coming.

The Surgeon has helped the Dancer to the top of the heap, her differently solid legs containing It (mirror-like) clocking different tones against metals, rocks, plastics, ceramics on the way up. They're atop a pile of everything, able to survey the columns and floors crumbling beyond where they're perched together. With The Surgeon's assistance, The Dancer has propped herself up against this final, bulky It, that is holding itself at the apex of the rest of the stuff. That such a hefty and foreboding item would make it up here, to the very top, should be surprising, but The Surgeon understands that without the usual organisational labels in place, anything can go anywhere.

It (lumpy) isn't a comfortable support for The Dancer, but nothing could be at this point.

It's time to labour.

The Dancer is resting her sacrum, lumber spine, shoulder blades, onto the It's extravagant outer face. Her skin meeting its almost wet exterior.

So much for the agile, euphoric – as was requested – miracle of birth, witnessing the onset of the warm-up contractions. The Surgeon knows that this thing is going to be rough.

> *I'm watching The Dancer as she attempts to repose, the closing of her eyes with each hunching over giving away the pain that she's trying to let pass through her and exit.*

Some seconds. The Dancer has never known her body in this way. A usually silent and dutiful inner organ is shouting out to her for help. This noisy thing within her compresses the small body that's turning within it, holds it there, squeezed, then returns to a softer-edged, but still mightily taut, form.

Some seconds. Another shift. The Dancer's body morphs to become cuboidal of its own accord, turns solid, sticks out jagged corners, brutal sides, clamps everything down, then eases back into a rounder space where it is possible to focus on other things. Some more seconds. Liquids that it's no longer necessary to hold in are forced out all over the floor, to gush out in new tides with each subsequent squeeze. The Surgeon knows that the yellow green tinge to the pool that's forming on the lino isn't the most hoped for colour in this scenario; she might have to get her hands dirty.

Then more corners, more re-gathering of breath, turgidity, releasing. Over and over.

Some hours now.

I'm empathising with the knowledge squashing inside my insides. That what will take place cannot be cropped and framed into a picture out in front but must be hurled up within without eyes describing it all down.

I'm leaving before the final crescendo.

The Surgeon squats by the labouring Dancer's legs, unsure whether she should adopt the role of supportive kin sitting to the side, or assured medic standing at the front.

The Dancer has belts strapped around her square stomach now. They've appeared from out of the stockpile and will be in place throughout to monitor the movements within, how fast, how regular, how strong, how hard, long, many. There's a ticker tape too noting it all down, all the hours and days of it, logging the chants and songs, and checking the scores for good change or bad change or just that time has passed. The data being noted out loud, real time, sending a monotone beep into space with every heartbeat, is deafening, but holds The Dancer in an embrace. The comforting cacophony of this temporary womb within the museum. No longer keeping its contents preserved and prioritising stillness, but breathing and squeezing with change. Her body performs its regular switches between hard cube and big egg for days on end, telling her each time that we need to feel this, we need to know that this is happening. Notice it harder, notice it more, notice it with squeezing hard enough to snap The Surgeon's finger you're gripping, with jaws clamped together like limpets clamped to rocks out of water. With everything you've got. And yet still not enough. Not enough signals to get this goddamn thing out. No secret code, no magic words to open the goddamn secret door.

OK.

Maybe too much noticing. Switch tactics. Go deep. Don't feel it as a thing feels a force being applied upon it, but as the force itself, moving as it does. Move as the surging (The Surgeon hates this term), crushing, fearing, birthing, alling, massiving force. Breathe as it does, slow, and in, and slow, and out. Breathe through it, through its lungs, into it, and out of it.

Just four more hours.

Four more hours has become the new single unit, and The Dancer must wait for one more new single unit to pass before she can progress to the next step. Four more hours of being slow, hunched over, facing inside, unable to lift herself away from It (lumpy) that's holding their weight and bracing her pains. Four more hours for The Surgeon to spend flitting between head and tail, body and book, heart and head.

The Dancer reaches the next milestone, the next unit, only to know that her next move is, yet again, to wait for four more hours to pass.

She can't do it anymore. The Dancer is done. Her body is always her first defence. Hours and days of training in sports halls and community centres, performances in town halls, nightclubs and on stages, stretching muscles to splitting point, working heart and lungs to their limits, and now being drilled from the inside, knocking her sense of self off balance in the wake. She can't birth this thing. She can't get it out of her.

Breathe.

Slowly.

There's a change in the pitch. She's brought inside herself to meet a different part of her body, feels a stinging hot stretch as the baby – The Dancer suddenly realises she's going to meet a baby – is pressing on now through her breathing, exposing every muscular part of her birth canal to the circumference of its vacuum-packed head.

Progress.

Descending.

The Surgeon helps The Dancer onto her knees, one hand gripping tight to the cold, hard It, the other clamped around The Surgeon's fingers, with the hope that gravity will help this new being fall out of her. Maybe it's going to come out on its own after all, and The Surgeon needn't think about the meconium in the waters, won't need to do anything other than be a pillar for gripping onto and a voice telling her to keep breathing slowly.

On and on they come and they go. The Dancer tries to feel her way through, to listen and respond to the contractions, pretending she knows what she's doing, hoping that she can listen attentively enough amidst the cacophony. A deep sinking push and The Surgeon sees the top of the baby's head. Another and the head meets the outside. Still attached and taking all its resources from The Dancer's body, the tiny death mask still has its eyes closed, isn't yet far enough out to have need for breathing.

It's almost done.

Breathing, and pushing, and squeezing, and deeply working from body and lungs and muscles and skins.

One last spasmodic storm and it's here. Birthed. Two separate entities on each end of a string.

It lives.

Plates

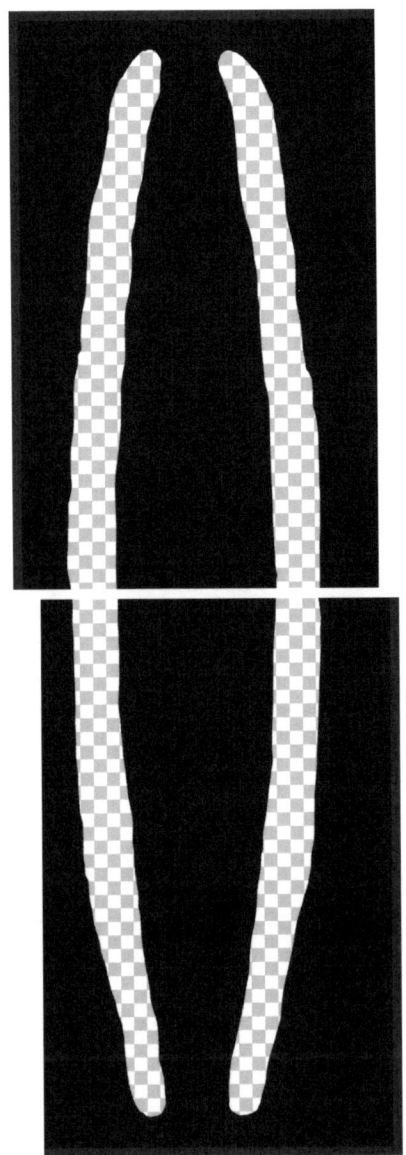

1

2

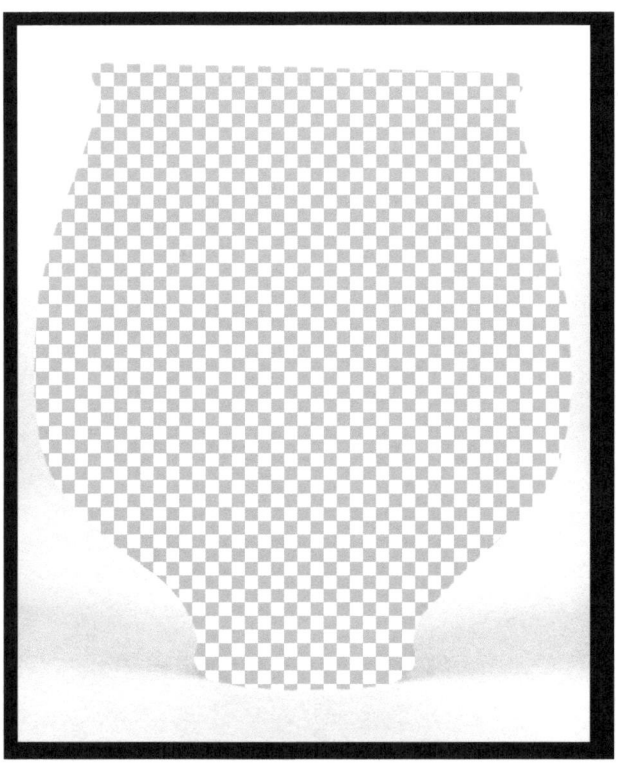

3

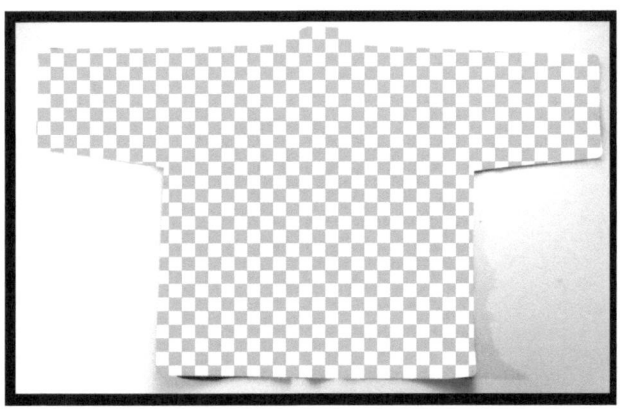

4

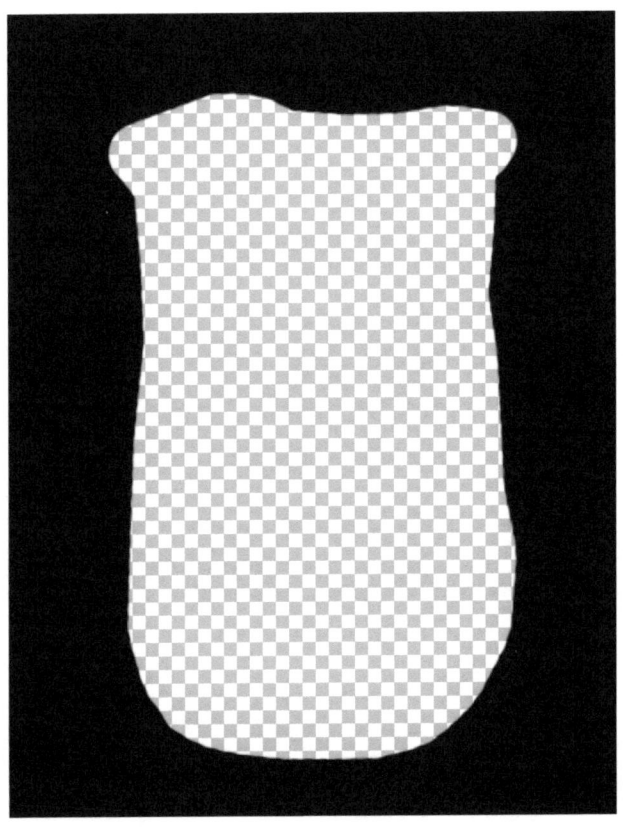

6

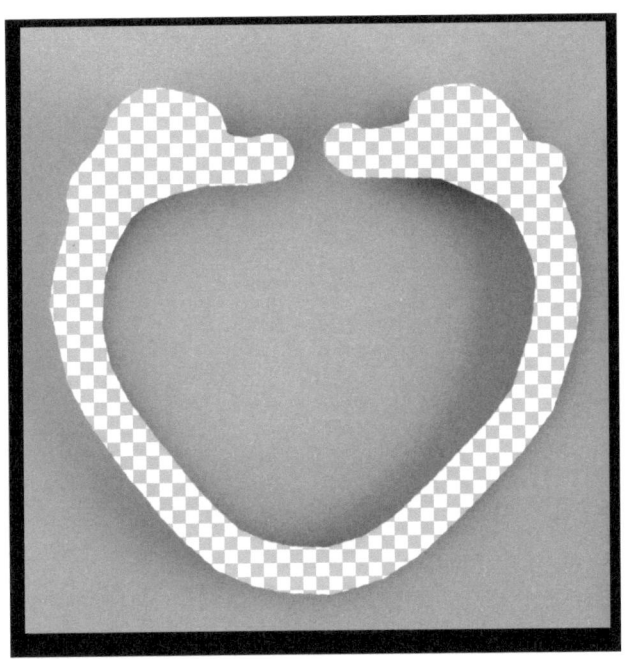

8

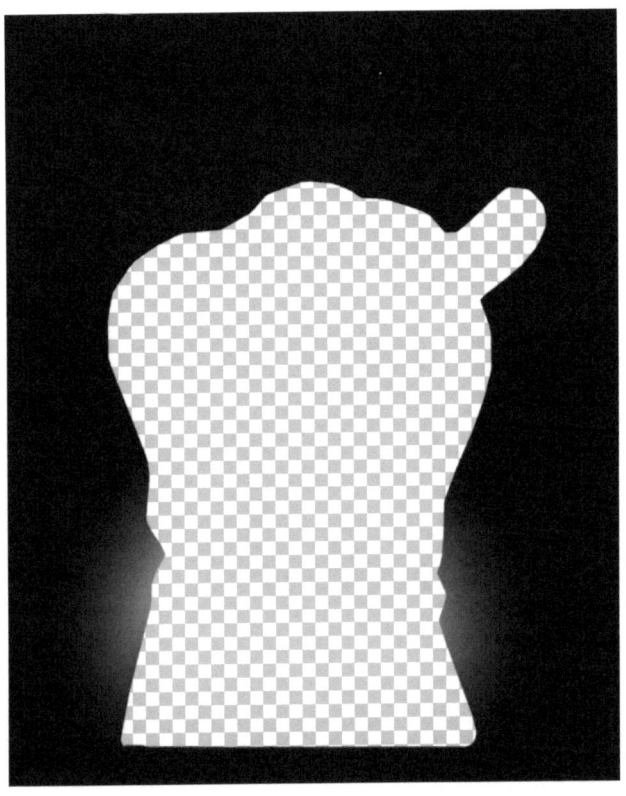

10

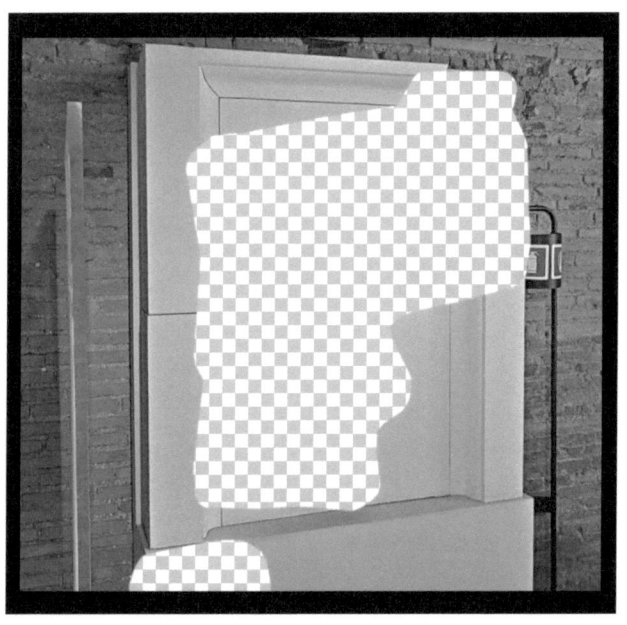

11

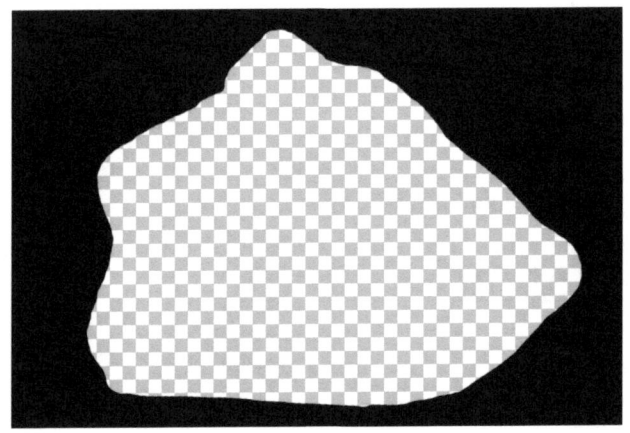

14

Object index

ambulances 47
ammonites, slices of 83
amputations 94
animal claw 74
antique gold 38
armchair 48
armoured plate 74
arrow 23
artificial limbs 42

bacon 51
balustrades, marble 83
batteries 60
beads 86
beetle, Golden tortoise 19
belts 102
bird(s) 30, 35, 78
   form 49
   's eye 35
blanket 36
blinds, semi-opaque 29
blinkers 39
blood, ruby of 44
bluebottle 29, 43
bone(s) 58, 61, 63, 64, 88, 89, 92, 97
   animal 60
   ankle 78
   broken 84
   dry 22
   jaw 78
   squashy 61
   wrist 66

book(s) 48, 49, 104
   flip 49
   pile of 50
   textbook 48, 50, 77
boots 94
box(es) 96
   wooden 85
brain 22, 67
bum filler 86
button(s) 60, 72

carpet squares, grey 17
carrier bag 32
carrot 76
cars 47
cat 76
caterpillar 91
ceramics 101
chair 11
club 59
coaster 47
coat 86
cocoon 91
coin(s) 60, 64
columns 101
computer 31
crisps, flecks of 61
crow's feet 12
cuboid of ice 91
cup of instant noodles 12
curtains 97
cushion 11

dentures 60
drawers 97

drawing of vegetation 96
dribble 22
dried cells, collection of 44
dust (particles)
   motes of 81
   sea of 33
   unit of 85

egg(s) 22, 103

false nails 60
fans 31
feather 38
   on a pond 43
fence panel 48
fire extinguisher 85
fluff 52
foam packing inserts 86
folder(s) 72
   yellow warning 23
foyer desk 8
freezer 53

giant signpost 49
glass cabinet 17
glasses, short-sight-correcting 58
glove 11
   disposable medical 14
   old 14
   rubber 11
   particular branded 32
grapes, in a bunch 26
hair 61

hair bobbles 92
hair grips 60
hammock 88
handle 12
headphone earbud 50
hologram 68
hoofs 94
horns 74

ice cube 90, 91
   human-shaped 91
ice sculptures 40
ice lolly 53
icing 62, 100

jigsaw 84

keyboard 61
keys 43, 58
   plastic 12
   set of 65

labels 34, 71, 97, 101
laptop 11, 23, 28, 31, 33, 47, 53, 72, 75, 77
leggings, wet 71
light beams 16
limpets 103
lino 102
liver, slice of 6
lollipop 80
lolly 53
lorries 47
lung 6

magnets 60
magpie 7
manatee 54
mandolin 13
map 35
marble(s) 60
    under rolled icing 62
mask(s)
    death 64, 74, 105
    golden sheet 86
mattress 48
meringue 83
microphone 50, 51, 52
mirror 88
    full-length 36
model of a body 33
modelled balloon poodle 80
mug 29, 47, 48, 52
    of tea 12
    slip-cast 47

nail(s) 42, 44, 56, 60, 76
needle 32
noodles 14

old money 38
old penny 56
ovaries 22
oyster 100

pacemakers 86
pants 96
paper 35
    volume of 48

pearl 100
peas 60
pen(s)
    black 86
    felt 86
    lids 60
pencil 35
phone case 86
pick-up sticks 88
pickle, in a jar 69
pillow 61
plates 97
plan chest 96
plinths 23
podium 42
poles 94
puppet 74
puppy 82

rat 35
real finger 12
ring 66
rocks 101, 103
ruler 47
sack 22
sand 80
sandwich 6
scab 43, 44
scale(s) 46, 74
scalpel 52
    non-sterile 47
scarecrow 30
screen 12, 23
    pop-up 6
screws 97

sea lion 54
shard of sunlight 33
sheet
   cleansed 32
   protective 97
shelf 35
shoes 96
shovel 23
skeleton 84, 88
skull 13, 22, 67, 77
sock, holding a foot 33
socket(s) 39
   plug 85
spikes, polished 94
spit droplets 28
splinter 48
spotlights 39
starlings, murmuration of 75
stick, wooden 53
stickleback 53
stones, calcified 83
studs 41
sugar 74

table 65, 66, 67
   operating 11, 12, 31, 33, 48, 61
tadpoles 10
Tannoy 16
taste buds 52, 53
teeth 60, 64, 72, 78
tepee 88
thread 32
   lengths of 97

ticker tape 103
tiles 41
   polished floor 83
titanium knee 85
toilet seat 67
tongue 27, 28, 34, 53, 54, 70, 71
   dismembered 52
   old 96
   piece of 28, 69
   section of severed 63
   severed 31, 70
tool(s) 34, 36, 50
   fine 64
   precision-cutting 27
   work 12
tooth 74
trainer 96
treasure chests 56

Victorian woodblock print of some grapes 96

warning bell 60, 78
woman's fist 48

xylophone 88

Acknowledgements

The seed of this work began with the support of an Engine Micro Bursary from New Art West Midlands and The New Art Gallery Walsall, via Walsall Council. Its development in the studio was funded by Arts Council England and its production made possible through backers via Kickstarter and An Endless Supply.

Joanne would like to thank: Ania Bas, for sharing feedback that lit the way to the next draft; Gavin Wade, for reading and encouraging early on; Paul Sammut, for offering insights and advice on realising the project; Robin Kirkham, for giving the work the perfect form, for eternal encouragement and for everything else; Jess Chandler, for posing careful questions, editing with expert sensitivity and supporting on all aspects of this thing that felt unknown; Felix and Ivan; and to everybody who invested in the work via Kickstarter.

Body of Pieces
Joanne Masding

Published by Bobo Books

Edited by Jess Chandler
Designed by An Endless Supply
Typeset in Rosart and Balance
Printed by TJ Books

ISBN 978 1 9160775 3 9
Copyright © Joanne Masding, 2024

All rights reserved. No part of this publication may be reproduced, copied or transmitted save with written permission from the publishers in accordance with the Copyright Designs and Patents Act, 1988

Bobo Books, Unit 3, Minerva Works
158 Fazeley Street, Birmingham B5 5RT

bobobooks.org